I0718757

Clean Regency Romance

Her Generous Duke

Arietta Richmond

Dreamstone Publishing © 2020

www.dreamstonepublishing.com

ISBN-13: 978-1-925915-85-3

Disclaimer

This is a work of fiction. Names, characters, places, organisations, events, and incidents are either products of the author's imagination or used fictitiously.

ARIETTA RICHMOND

Dedication

For everyone who had the grace to be patient while this book, and every other book that I have written, was coming into existence, who provided cups of tea, and food, when the writing would not let me go, and endured countless times being asked for opinions.

For the readers who inspire me to continue writing, by buying my books! Especially for those of you who have taken the time to email me, or to leave reviews, and tell me what you love about my books, and what you'd like to see more of – thank you – I'm listening. I hope that you enjoy book, just as much as my other books.

For my growing team of beta readers and advance reviewers – it's thanks to you that others can enjoy these books in the best presentation possible!

And for all the writers of Regency Historical Romance, whose books I read, who inspired me to write in this fascinating period.

Table of Contents

Books by Arietta Richmond

His Majesty's Hounds

Claiming the Heart of a Duke

Giving a Heart of Lace

Enchanting the Duke

Finding the Duke's Heir

Healing Lord Barton

Loving the Bitter Baron

Rescuing the Countess

Attracting the Spymaster

Intriguing the Viscount

Being Lady Harriet's Hero

Redeeming the Marquess

Winning the Merchant Earl

Kissing the Duke of Hearts

Falling for the Earl

Betting on a Lady's Heart

Courting a Spinster for Christmas

Restoring the Earl's Honour

From Soldier Spy to Lord (contains the first three books in one volume)

To Love a Determined Lady (Contains Books 4, 5 and 6 in one volume)

Love Heals a Lord (Contains Books 7, 8 and 9 in one volume)

To Love a Dashing Lord (Contains Books 10, 11, 12, and 13 in one volume)

For a Lady's Honour (Contains Books 14, 15, 16, and 17 in one volume)

A Duke's Daughters – The Elbury Bouquet

A Spinster for a Spy (Lily)

A Bluestocking for a Baron (Rose)

A Vixen for a Viscount (Hyacinth)

A Diamond for a Duke (Camellia)

A Minx for a Merchant (Primrose)

An Enchantress for an Earl (Violet) (coming soon)

A Maiden for a Marquess (Iris) (coming soon)

A Heart for an Heir (Thorne) (coming soon)

The Nettlefold Chronicles

The Duke and the Spinster

A Duke in Autumn

To Dance with the Dangerous Duke

A Christmas Bride for the Duke

The Regency Gothic Series

Lord of the Storm

Lord of the Darkness

Lord of the Lost (coming soon)

Lord of the Shadows (coming soon)

Lady Canterford's Conspirators (The Mayfair Ladies Poetry Society)

A six book series (coming soon)

The Regency Scandals Series

The Gift of a Christmas Scandal
Lady Mariel's Scandalous Love
Christmas with *That* Duke

The Derbyshire Set

A Gift of Love (Prequel short story)
A Devil's Bargain (Prequel short story - coming soon)
The Earl's Unexpected Bride
The Captain's Compromised Heiress
The Viscount's Unsuitable Affair
The Count's Impetuous Seduction
The Rake's Unlikely Redemption
The Marquess' Scandalous Mistress
A Remembered Face (Bonus short story – coming soon)
The Marchioness' Second Chance
A Viscount's Reluctant Passion
Lady Theodora's Christmas Wish
The Duke's Improper Love (coming soon)
A Gentleman's Unconventional Courtship (coming soon)
The Derbyshire Set, Omnibus Edition, Volume 1 (the first three books in one volume.)
The Derbyshire Set, Omnibus Edition, Volume 2 (the second three books in one volume.)

Other Books

The Scottish Governess
Her Summer Duke
Her Passionate Duke
Her Absent Duke
Her Determined Duke
Her Generous Duke
The Duke's Christmas Vow
Her Christmas Duke (Coming Soon)
The Crew of the Seadragon's Soul Series, (coming soon - a set of 10 linked novels)

Themed Collections

The Regency Christmas Hearts Collection
The Regency Spring and Valentine's Hearts Collection
The Regency Summer Hearts Collection
The Regency Autumn Hearts Collection

ARIETTA RICHMOND

x

Chapter One

"Hope, dear cousin, tell me – what do you know how to do? I must gain an understanding of your accomplishments, so that I will know what else you need to learn."

Lady Hope Spencer had regarded her cousin, Evelyn, Countess of Mainthorpe, with wide uncertain eyes, and stuttered her reply.

"Do?"

"Do. Such as paint watercolours, play the pianoforte, dance a variety of common dances, eat with the proper etiquette, embroider delicate pictures, and the like."

Even now, three years later, Hope still recalled the horror she, at fifteen, had felt at her cousin's words. For she had known how to do precisely none of those things at all. She had Evelyn to thank for the fact that she could, at this moment, claim some respectable ability in all of them.

Which fact did not ease her nervousness, now, one whit.

Hope glanced up as the carriage jolted to a stop. She caught her cousin's eye, which was not devoid of compassion - however coddling was never Evelyn's way, and she merely nodded at Hope encouragingly as she stepped out of the carriage. Hope nearly forgot to grasp the hand of the footman who opened the door, but she remembered in time to be helped out. She felt so nervous that she feared she would even forget how to breathe.

The sun was setting, although it wasn't quite completely dark - dusk was falling, and the few gas lamps lining the street illuminated the young women in lovely dresses in white and pastel and the men in sharply tailored tailcoats and hats. A thrill ran through Hope's body at the realisation that she was finally at the kind of Ball she had dreamed of attending for so long. Now that she was here, though, the fear of a misstep made her want to be back home. She took a shaking breath and tried to calm her mounting nerves. This would be her first Ball, her introduction to society – and even three years of instruction and preparation suddenly seemed totally inadequate.

'Everything will go well,' she repeated, over and over, in her thoughts.

They descended from the carriage, and joined the long line of people waiting to enter. Hope looked at the beautifully dressed, whispering girls ahead of her, who all seemed to know each other. *'See? These girls can do this.'* But those girls were not coming out into society for the first time, like she was, most likely – they would have been to Balls before. In that moment, Hope felt far younger than she was, inexperienced, and as a result a knot clenched in her stomach as she imagined all of the possible humiliating mistakes she might make: tripping over her hem, bumping into someone important, being too shy and awkward to make polite conversation – or even worse.

She swallowed nervously and wrenched her eyes away from the confidently chattering competition and focussed on her gloved hands. That was what the other girls were, after all - competition. At least, that's what her cousin Evelyn told her. Her mind went back to the beginning, three years before, when she had first gone to visit Evelyn at Mainthorpe Hall.

She could hear Evelyn's words, the first day that she'd begun to teach Hope in her parlour, in her mind, now.

"Now, Hope, remember. However well the other young ladies dance, draw, play, speak, sing, or look – you must do it better."

Which simply made her more nervous, again.

Although Evelyn and Hope were cousins, Evelyn was the elder by twelve years – as a result of which, the two hadn't spent much time together when Hope was growing up, for Evelyn had married when Hope was just six years old.

Evelyn's mother, Dahlia, Hope's aunt, was a sharp tongued, iron willed woman who did not get on very well with her sister, Hope's mother Alice, and had barely stayed in contact when she married and moved to the next county over. In her haste to be away from the family home, she had married the first man who offered – a Baron of reasonable reputation, but little wealth.

Her daughter, Evelyn, had grown up more quick-witted than her mother - Evelyn, Hope's mother had commented often in a wry voice, was a shrewd woman. She had managed, at sixteen, to attract the sponsorship of a great aunt, and gone to London to live with her, where she had learned the mannerisms, affectations, and fashions of the upper echelon of society.

She had attracted the attention of the Earl of Mainthorpe, and married him at the end of her first Season.

Theirs was an affectionate relationship, even though it had not been a love match. Now, she hoped to help her young cousin do as well as she had – for which Hope was very grateful.

Much had changed in the three years since Evelyn had first contacted her, and suggested that she might help – first her father's death, then the revelation of the depth of debt he had left them in, and then her mother's failing health.

Hope needed to do well - needed, ideally, to find a wealthy man to marry, to save herself and her mother from impending destitution. They had one small estate, and everything else had gone to a cousin when her father, the Earl of Salenton, had died.

The line moved forward, and Hope pulled her thoughts back to the present.

Surely, if Evelyn had carved a future for herself out of a less than ideal family situation, so could Hope. She glanced at Evelyn, beside her. At thirty, Evelyn still held the charm and poise of a much younger person, though a sardonically arched brow betrayed her mature view on life from wisdom gained over the years. Years in which the only cause for sadness was the fact that she had never quickened with child.

Hope found herself wondering dolefully if Evelyn would truly be able to manufacture such a future for her. It would be so easy if she were only as sparkling, vibrant, and outgoing as her cousin. Evelyn was worldly, witty, and an expert at making the most of her assets. Hope was, even after all of Evelyn's efforts at teaching her, quite the opposite.

The line moved again, and they reached the steps. Hope allowed her thoughts to drift back into memories, if only to distract herself from how very nervous she felt about what would happen once they stepped into the ballroom.

For the first year, as Evelyn began to teach her everything she would need to know to do well in society, Hope had been, if rather overwhelmed, also hopeful. But her father's shocking death had destroyed that growing confidence, and forced her to learn far more about the exigencies of life than any girl should have to at sixteen.

For her father had been, for years, steadily gambling away their fortunes, and hiding that fact from his wife. As he lost more, so he drank more, and therefore made more rash decisions and lost more again.

The day that he was brought home on a hurdle, after having been found dead in an alley behind a gaming hell in the nearby town, was the day that her mother's health began to decline – and the day that Hope became, in lieu of there being anyone else to do so, mistress of the house in her mother's place.

She looked around at the chattering young women nearby, and wondered if any of them had ever had to face such things, or if the costs and complexities of running a household were things which waited in their futures, and had not yet ever been spared a thought.

Oh, to have not had to face it herself!

But she had.

Evelyn had helped Hope, as she and her mother were forced to move from Salenton Grange into the far smaller Cherrywood Manor, to hire what few servants they could afford, and to establish, with their man of business, Mr Jenkins, Hope's authority to act on her mother's behalf.

It had been challenging, especially as they realised how little money they had. Hope felt, in some ways, many years older than the girls around her, and in other ways, much younger.

The biggest challenge at the time had been managing to continue her lessons with Evelyn, but her mother had insisted that she do so, that their hope for the future rested on her shoulders – so lessons had continued, although reduced to once a week instead of every day.

In her turn, Evelyn increased the intensity of that weekly lesson, packing many concepts into one lesson so that Hope sometimes felt that she would drop from the pressures of maintaining a household and improving her social skills.

Finally, a few months ago, as Hope had turned eighteen, Evelyn was at last unable to criticise anything Hope had done during a lesson. All she said, though, was that Hope was now 'fit to be seen'. Despite her cousin's calculating exterior, Hope knew that she could trust Evelyn, and had often confided in her sympathetic, if critical, ear.

The line moved again, and they reached the top of the steps.

"Remember, dear," Evelyn murmured as they stepped through the door of the impressive townhouse. The Ball was being hosted by the Lord Tartington, an extremely wealthy and influential man. Hope felt like her eyes would pop out of her head as she craned her neck back to stare at the five storied townhome, but a gentle bump of Evelyn's elbow reminded her to straighten her neck and close her gaping mouth. Evelyn resumed her lecture. "Remember to *whom* you are to speak, and to *whom* you are *not*."

It wasn't as though Hope would be above speaking to anyone at the Tartington's Ball – goodness, no.

On the contrary, Evelyn had reminded Hope countless times that she was simply not in the position to speak to most people attending the Ball that night.

Speaking to anyone, but especially those of higher rank, required an introduction, and Hope was well aware that *her* misstep could mean a blot on her mentor's reputation.

Hope cast aside thoughts of the past, and of everything that depended on her doing well, and put all of her effort into being as charming as she could as she curtsied to the host and hostess, kept her hands demurely in front of her, and followed Evelyn to a corner of the ballroom without tripping or otherwise disgracing herself.

Grateful to have navigated things to that point successfully, Hope let out a loud breath of relief. Evelyn shot her a look and Hope sealed her lips, certain that, no matter what she did, she could never look as beautiful as the girls around her.

****

Xavier Harte, Duke of Birkchester, regarded his friend, James, Marquess of Ashton, with some annoyance.

"You need not remind me, Ashton – the matter weighs on my mind badly enough as it is."

"Then do something about it, Birkchester. The Season is beginning – there will be dozens of fresh young things – all of whom would be delighted to be a Duchess – just waiting to be chosen by a man. You are, by their accounting, quite the catch – so talk to them, and pick one who appeals."

They moved forward in the damnably long receiving line for the Ball they were about to enter, and Xavier shook his head.

"There may be dozens of hopefuls who would love to be a Duchess – but they are the ones I want to avoid – those ones are all about greed and a desire to be important – I would prefer a woman who would be happy with a quieter life, someone I might share interests with, someone I might actually like…"

"Come now, Birkchester, that's a bit optimistic of you! If you are to ever get yourself an heir, you'll need to choose a woman to marry – and I doubt that any young woman of the *ton* will be interested in living a quiet life in the country. You'll have to compromise somewhere in your list of requirements."

Xavier shook his head, and they let the conversation drop as they reached the top of the stairs and stepped in to greet their host. But Ashton's words stayed in Xavier's mind as they separated, and each moved about the ballroom, greeting people they knew. He was tempted to simply retreat to the card room, but forced himself not to – he would never find a woman to marry unless he spoke to them, and danced with them.

He moved across the room, greeting friends, until he reached a corner, not far from the doors onto the terrace. There, he leant casually against a pillar, and watched the room, assessing which young women were present that he had met before, and who there was that he had not. He was just about to turn away, to go in search of a drink, annoyed that he had yet to see anyone new, when the crowds shifted, and two women came into the room.

One, he had seen at various Balls – she was older, married to Mainthorpe, if he remembered aright – but the one with her was younger, and he'd never seen her before. Her hair was a glossy red-gold, like a fine chestnut horse, and she looked around as if quite overwhelmed, her pretty face anxious.

Who was she?

Chapter Two

Hope felt flustered as Evelyn introduced her to two older ladies, who made positive comments about her gown, which was enough to make her blush. Internally she bemoaned her pale complexion, which was a perfect canvas for every embarrassed feeling to be displayed. Hope had inherited almost all of the features of her mother, except for her father's wide mouth. She had a slender build and medium height, with rich red-gold hair, bright green eyes, and a scattering of freckles. It was a distinctive appearance – more noticeable than most, with her bright hair, and she thought, in that moment, that she would have been happier had she been of more ordinary colouring.

Growing up, Hope had felt very plain and unremarkable. Although her body hadn't developed the voluptuous curves of many of her peers, she had grown to be well proportioned and attractive, if not classically beautiful. Of late Evelyn had commented multiple times on the charms of her appearance, although Hope had difficulty believing that Evelyn could possibly be serious.

On the one hand, her cousin was not one to give compliments lightly, so perhaps she was truly pretty. On the other hand, her cousin's goal was to draw Hope out of her shell, so it could just be a ploy to build her confidence.

In any case, thus far there had been few opportunities in Hope's repetitive, cloistered life to meet attractive young men, and she felt unusually hot and bothered standing in the fashionable ballroom, surrounded by gentlemen of the nobility. A couple of men standing nearby, who were dressed in the latest stare of fashion, and quite good to look upon, were giving her appreciative glances which left no doubt as to their admiration.

Hope blushed all the brighter, and quickly cast her eyes away from the men, realising that, although she was not naturally all that large of bosom, her new ballgown, set over her well-constructed stays, certainly created that illusion. She looked around, taking in the array of people in the room, trying to distract herself from the regard of the nearby men.

People shifted, and, through the crowd, suddenly, Hope's eyes met another pair of eyes across the room. The deep-set eyes were somewhere between hazel and brown, a colour like the water of a forest pool in spring, she thought, and their owner had a well-defined chin, with expressive facial features. For that moment, it was as if all else faded away a little, and she was sinking into those eyes.

She immediately looked away, feeling a deep crimson blush creep over her cheeks and neck, and she wryly wondered why her whole body didn't just turn red and be done with it. Unable to stop herself, she surreptitiously took another glance at the man, who had by now turned his attention elsewhere. He was tall, with wide shoulders and thick black hair which lay in well-groomed order upon his head.

"Now dear, just remember that there will be those I will introduce you to, and those who we will *not* be talking to," Evelyn said next to her, lowering her voice and fluttering her fan demurely in front of her mouth. "That," she indicated the man that Hope had just been looking at, "is Xavier Harte, the Duke of Birkchester. The highest we can expect to aim for you is a Viscount, or perhaps an Earl, so we will not be talking to him, no matter how handsome he is. I will not have you setting your cap at a man who is not likely to consider you – a Duke can have his pick of all of the young ladies, and is like to choose the highest ranked, or the most beautiful – because he can. If, however, he should seek an introduction..."

Hope blushed in embarrassment before realising that her cousin was just teasing her. In spite of her cousin's well-meaning efforts, the night was still a trial for Hope. She was not very outgoing – she loved reading, drawing, and enjoying nature. Balls were an entirely different experience from her daily life. For the last two years, when she had not been learning from Evelyn, she had been concentrating on learning how to manage a household, a small estate, and an impossible tangle of debt and ever diminishing money. The purpose of a Ball, however, was to see and be seen, to display one's wealth and beauty, without a care for how anything in the world was managed or paid for. The women around her seemed to glow from the enjoyment of gossip, flirting, and dancing, while Hope just wanted to be quiet and alone.

The people Evelyn introduced her to weren't the sort that Hope would usually seek out, either. Fashionable London society was not too varied - Hope felt as though she were meeting the same woman over and over again. That woman was sparkling, trying to act with confidence, and to be witty, as she flitted about with a bright smile, laughing and flirting to her heart's content.

Hope felt the condescension in the ladies' voices as they were introduced and said, *'delightful to meet you, Lady Hope,'* while smiling pityingly with arched eyebrows. Although Hope highly doubted that the ladies knew the truth behind her father's disgraceful death, it was apparent that enough was rumoured of her lack of fortune, deceased father, and most likely reduced circumstances to make her an object of 'charitable pity' for many. Hope was soon feeling rather annoyed, and tired from pretending to be as impressed by the other ladies as she was clearly expected to be - Evelyn was used to such politics, but Hope had never been good at prevaricating.

Nonetheless, the gentlemen still seemed interested in her, and she danced three times, with various men she found, at close quarters, rather unimpressive. At least she managed to dance the steps correctly, and to not step on their toes. When the third dance finished, and the gentleman delivered her back to Evelyn, they went in search of refreshment.

As they walked about, drinks in hand, she whispered to Evelyn that she wished desperately for some straightforward and good-natured people to speak with. Evelyn laughed, and patted her hand, but Hope sighed in relief when Evelyn then said that they should begin their goodbyes. They circulated, sipping as they went, and the superior ladies smiled falsely and expressed the desire to see Hope at other social occasions, but Hope was quite sure that they did not mean it. Secretly she felt that she wouldn't be at all sad if it was quite a while before her next Ball.

With relief, Hope realised, as she followed Evelyn, that they were approaching the exit from the ballroom. She still held the half empty glass of wine in her hand – Evelyn had passed off her own glass to a footman long since - and she tried to get her cousin's attention, unsure what to do with the glass.

But Evelyn was moving rapidly in and out of the remaining people who were between them and the door. Glass still in hand, Hope hurried to catch up to her cousin, and was just about to touch her arm when someone turned suddenly beside her. An elbow swung towards her own arm, and despite her best efforts to avoid the collision, she watched her wine fly out of the glass and splash onto the person attached to that elbow.

Everything seemed to move in slow motion as Hope took in the surprised and offended expressions of the people who surrounded her, the dismay on Evelyn's face as she turned back for her charge, and finally, a shirt and cravat stained with wine. With a sense of dread, Hope's eyes travelled upward until they found the recipient of her clumsiness – Xavier Harte, Duke of Birkchester.

If Hope had blushed before, it was nothing to what she was doing now.

"I – I – I beg your pardon," Hope stuttered, feeling as though she might faint at any moment. "I apologise for my clumsiness."

Wine dripped from the Duke's front onto the floor as the young women nearby tittered and whispered.

Evelyn rushed over and apologised profusely.

"I am *so* sorry, Your Grace. If I might introduce my cousin, Lady Hope Spencer. It was just a little mistake, I'm sure – please forgive her, we were hurrying and I am certain that she meant no harm."

As she spoke, Evelyn put a hand on Hope's arm and looked significantly from her to the Duke. By this time several footmen had whipped out cloths and offered them, but the Duke waved them away and used his own handkerchief to mop himself dry. All the while, his eyes remained fixed on Hope.

"I am very sorry."

Hope finally murmured earnestly, hoping that by apologising again, she might somehow make the whole incident not have happened.

She met the Duke's gaze. His hazel eyes seemed to be peering into her soul, and a shiver went through her, in a way that she had never felt before.

He seemed to be about to say something when Evelyn curtsied, again, speaking rapidly, obviously desperate to remove them from the scene and avoid any further notice from the gossips.

"Forgive us, Your Grace, but we must depart."

She hurried away, pulling Hope with her.

Behind her, the Duke still stood, watching them go, a curious expression on his face.

When they were safely tucked away in the carriage, a single tear fell down Hope's face as her cousin sat next to her.

"There, there, you mustn't cry. It wasn't so bad for your first Ball."

"I spilled wine on a Duke! The gossip will tear me apart for that clumsiness," Hope sobbed, "my Season is over, I suppose."

"Now, now, don't make such a muddle of it," Evelyn said sympathetically, putting an arm around her cousin. "Mistakes happen all the time. I'm sure that no one thought that you spilled your drink on purpose – they all saw that the Duke turned in the crowded space, and collided with you. Now, dry your eyes and rest well tonight, and you'll see in the morning that things didn't go so badly tonight. I'm sure that you'll never see His Grace up close again, and that will be that."

✴✴✴✴✴

Xavier waved the fussing footmen away. His valet would curse him tonight – and so he should, for it had been his own fault. He had been the one who had turned without consideration for the crowd, and collided with the young lady. She had apologised profusely, her face flushed with embarrassment, but he had been caught by the genuine nature of that apology, by the manner in which she had seemed far more interested in escaping the Ball than in attempting to intrigue him.

Many a young woman he had met would have taken the opportunity to simper, to 'faint' from the shock of it, or do anything else they could think of to place the blame on someone else, and attempt to get him to 'save' them. That the girl – what was the name the older woman had given? – Lady Hope Spencer? – had done none of that, but had immediately taken all blame on herself astounded him.

That she was very pretty in a most unusual way had also had an impact on him. Her eyes were a bright green, like leaves in spring, and the pale green of her gown had made them seem to glow. He wanted to know more about her. The wine on his clothes was irrelevant – his valet would clean them, or if they were uncleanable, he could easily afford more – but the woman who had spilled it… she was far more of interest. Because she was different, in so many ways.

For the first time, since he had begun to consider it time to choose a wife, a seed of hope had been planted in him. There was something about her… some sense that she might be as unenthused about large Balls as he was, for a start.

He had seen her, across the room, quite early in the night, but after that she had been rather reclusive – he had only noticed her again the few times that she had danced, and then she had slipped back into the shadows. He had already been a little intrigued before the wine incident – now, he was more so.

He wanted to know more about her.

Which thought, all by itself, was rather shocking. Perhaps he would ask some questions, quietly, and discover what he could.

✷✷✷✷✷

"Smith, I'd like a report on these three investments. I've the impression that it is, perhaps, time to withdraw from these and put my money where it can do more good. These looked to have good potential, but I'm beginning to suspect that the promised returns won't be happening."

"Yes, Your Grace – I'll look into it – I'll get my preferred investigator to check all of the companies' recent dealings, and then prepare the report for you."

"Excellent. Also, please do a little research for me – I would like to know what you can discover about the family of Lady Hope Spencer."

The man of business raised an eyebrow at the request, but simply bowed.

"As you wish, Your Grace."

Chapter Three

A week later, Hope had recovered from her embarrassment and was able to laugh at herself and finally enjoy London.

There was a lot of hustle and bustle, a lot to see, and so many new people to meet – even if she did miss the quiet countryside and the clear air of her home. At the same time, it was her first extended period of time away, and she enjoyed the temporary freedom from the tiring duties of home, and helping her mother.

When Hope had hesitated to come to London, Evelyn had, with typical generosity, hired a rather redoubtable woman to be companion to Hope's mother, and ensure that everything necessary still got done.

"I do hope mother will be able to manage with just two servants, and Mrs Stoughton," Hope said one Sunday morning over breakfast. She looked down guiltily at the ham and eggs she was about to consume with enthusiasm. "After all, she isn't well, and if something were to happen..."

"Now, don't be worrying about that," her cousin said reprovingly over the fruit basket. "My aunt is an intelligent and capable woman, and would not have let her daughter leave home if she couldn't spare her. And Mrs Stoughton will take good care of her – she's a very kind and reliable woman. After all, your mother wanted you to come here! You had to come out into society eventually, you know – and the sooner the better. Now, no more dour thoughts. You've only been gone a bit more than a week. I'm sure nothing has changed at home."

Hope nodded and smiled, brushing her fears away. Since her father had died, it had been just her and her mother, alone, but for two servants – an abnormal, if not precarious situation for two women to be in. They didn't have much family, and when Evelyn had offered to take them in, Hope's mother had insisted on staying in their own house – her pride driving her to retain her independence. But since then, her illness had advanced, and now, she was mostly bedridden - and no one yet had the will to insist on moving her, so for the past year a nurse who came in twice a week, and two servants, were all that the Spencers could afford.

After breakfast, Hope found herself still worrying about her mother, even as she put on her bonnet and stepped into the carriage to go to church. When she worried about her mother and their finances, a cloud inevitably fell over her as she was reminded of the intense pressure she carried - the responsibility of marrying well to lift her mother and herself out of destitution. Would she be able to do it? Entice some rich man to marry her?

After seeing the wiles and flirting skills of the young women at the Ball, Hope doubted it. After all, what did she have to offer?

Neither riches, beauty, nor wittiness.

She was entirely too harsh on herself, however. If someone had been asked about her attributes as she stepped out of the carriage before the church a few minutes later, an entirely different judgement may have been delivered than the one she herself had pronounced. Her petite figure, wide green eyes and red-gold hair were not the ideal standards of Grecian beauty so popular at the moment, but she held a charm of her own which she didn't yet recognise.

The two women walked up the church steps, amongst what felt like all of London society. Hope didn't immediately recognise anyone from the Ball, but resolved to swallow any lingering embarrassment and smile and nod at everyone, just in case.

The service was uneventful, but she enjoyed it. It was a rare chance to be both quiet and meditative, and also to observe the people around her. Her eyes scanned the fashionable London crowd, and marvelled at how beautifully they were dressed. Not only was she surrounded by delicate or handsome finery, but the vicar's sermon was decidedly different from the ones she was used to at home. Hope's usual vicar was sleepy and mild, while this vicar was fervent, energetic, and stern. She felt quite invigorated by his denouncing of immoral popular lifestyles and habits, and she sat up straighter in her chair as she observed the slightly guilty countenances of her neighbours.

"That was quite the sermon, was it not?" Evelyn asked as they made their leisurely way back out of the church, to where the elaborate gowns, hats and parasols of fine ladies were on display in the bright sun as they stopped to chatter.

It seemed that, in London, any chance to see, and be seen, was taken.

"Quite," Hope agreed, a smile tugging at her lips.

She was sure that the vicar had meant to prick the consciences of many of the Lords and Ladies in his congregation.

"Oh, I do beg your pardon," a deep voice suddenly said as Hope felt someone brush against her arm.

The owner of the voice turned, and Hope was horrified to see that it was the Duke of Birkchester. He looked at her quite curiously, and didn't seem at all angry or annoyed to see her; which was surprising, given the humiliating circumstance of their last meeting.

"Your Grace," Evelyn murmured as the two women sank into curtsies. "Come along, Hope, and take care not to bump anyone else."

The Duke looked around, quickly ducked away, and caught up to the two women a moment later with the vicar in tow.

"Lady Mainthorpe," the stately vicar said, bowing to Evelyn and gesturing to the Duke, "may I formally introduce you to His Grace of Birkchester."

Evelyn curtsied again, caught by the requirements of propriety, and unable to rush away. The vicar smiled benignly, and left, evidently feeling that he had completed his duty by performing the introductions.

Hope curtsied too, and the Duke bowed to both of them. Then, silence fell. Hope felt very uncertain, and glanced nervously at Evelyn, who was looking rather agitated. Finally, Evelyn spoke, breaking the silence.

"Your Grace, this is my cousin, Lady Hope Spencer, who you met, informally and briefly, at a Ball last week. She is staying with me in London."

Hope noted with surprise that the Duke was gazing at her with some intensity.

She noticed again just how pleasant an appearance he presented. Those deep hazel eyes held hers, and for a moment, she was aware of nothing else.

"It is good to have now been formally introduced," Evelyn enthused, as she put her hand on Hope's arm, "But we really must be going – here is our carriage now. Come along, Hope." She gave another curtsey, and motioned Hope to do the same, then almost tugged Hope away. As the two women left the Duke behind them, Hope was quite certain that he had been about to speak again. "*Most* peculiar," Evelyn muttered as she ushered Hope into the carriage.

"It was nice of the Duke to wish to be formally introduced to us, was it not?" Hope ventured hesitantly.

"Certainly," her cousin said, arranging her skirt and gloves restlessly. "The question is why."

Hope stared out of the window as they rattled back to the townhouse, a slight smile on her lips. Evelyn didn't seem to think it possible that the Duke may have wanted to talk to Hope, so she simply tried to put it out of her mind – she didn't really care why the Duke had gone out of his way to be introduced to a Lady of a lower rank, and her disenfranchised cousin. But she did, she found, hope that she might see him again. There was just something about him...

Xavier watched the two women walk away, feeling torn between amusement and annoyance. He had hoped for a longer conversation... but it was not to be – not today, anyway.

It was as if the older woman had something against him, as if she was trying to protect her young cousin from him. Perhaps she was, although for the life of him, he couldn't work out why – his reputation was boringly respectable, and most chaperones were all too ready to throw their young charges in his path, in the hope that he might be fool enough to marry them.

He shook his head, annoyed with himself now. For he should be considering marrying them, rather than avoiding them. And now, the first time that he had seen a woman he actually found interesting – because she seemed different, because she was not casting herself in his path, it was as if she had no wish to be anywhere near him. But perhaps that was still the lingering embarrassment caused by the incident with the glass of wine at the Ball.

Nonetheless, whatever the reason for it, it made her far more intriguing – because, surely, everything about her actions suggested that she did not simply view him as a possible source of wealth and position in society. Might it be possible… that she actually saw him, as a man, not a path to being a Duchess?

If she did, then perhaps she might be the solution to his problem. He felt an odd affinity for her, that sense he'd had when he'd very first seen her across the ballroom, that she would rather be somewhere else, somewhere quieter. That character, that lack of desire for grand social occasions, was exactly what he hoped for in a woman to be his wife.

He should call on her. If he spent some time talking to her, he might confirm his impression of her, might discover if she truly was a good possibility as a wife.

He had not yet heard back from Smith, but it had only been a few days – and he did not think it likely that there would be any scandal attached to the girl. She seemed far too retiring to be the sort to attract trouble.

He turned, as his carriage drew up before the church, and walked to it, ignoring the fluttering of the young women he passed – barely aware of them, in fact. His mind turned the idea over. Lady Hope Spencer might well save him from an interminable Season of simpering young women.

Later this week, he would definitely call on her, and see how she reacted. And, if she still seemed as quiet and inoffensive a young lady as he hoped, perhaps he would throw caution to the winds, and ask her… the question….

Just the thought sent a shiver of uncertainty through him, but he firmed his resolve – he needed a wife.

✳✳✳✳✳

'Again' turned out to be sooner than Hope had thought. A week later, the butler interrupted the two women just as Evelyn and Hope were in the middle of a quiet afternoon tea.

"Pardon me, my Lady, but a gentleman is here to see you."

He proffered a calling card on the tray.

"A gentleman? To see me?" Evelyn raised an eyebrow, even as she lifted the card. "But I'm not expecting anyone." She turned her eyes to the card, and Hope watched as they widened. "Oh, my! It's the Duke of Birkchester, Hope."

"The Duke? Here?"

Hope heard the slight quaver in her own voice. Evelyn set her teacup down a little too forcefully.

"Well!" Evelyn composed herself quickly. "We mustn't keep His Grace waiting. Dobson, show him in – and send for a fresh tea tray." Evelyn turned to Hope with an annoyed expression and muttered, "I never! With no warning, not even a note sent in advance. I've never heard of such a thing."

Hope wondered, yet again, why Evelyn seemed quite so determined that the Duke should not have any interest in Hope. Surely, most women who sponsored a young lady into society dreamed of her attracting the attention of a Duke?

"His Grace, the Duke of Birkchester."

Dobson delivered the announcement rather portentously, Hope thought. As the Duke stepped into the room, Evelyn's face had quickly changed from irritation to an expression of gracious solicitousness. Hope rose, beside Evelyn, and curtsied to the Duke, who bowed elegantly. Evelyn indicated the couches and chairs.

"Do be seated Your Grace. I have called for tea. To what do we owe the honour of you calling upon us?"

They all sank onto the seats, and Hope found herself beside the Duke on one of the couches. So close up, his presence was rather overwhelming – he was a tall man, with a strong well shaped body, and was, now she saw him again, even more handsome than she had thought him at first sight. He had a rather serious expression, with steady eyes, and a firm mouth. He was impeccably dressed, and held himself with a rod-straight back.

She studied him under lowered lashes as he spoke to Evelyn of the weather, and the social events which were planned for the next week or so.

A maid brought in the fresh tea tray, and Evelyn served him tea.

He took it, and sipped, then, taking advantage of the lull in the conversation caused by the tea, the Duke turned his large hazel eyes directly onto Hope. She blushed to the roots of her red-gold hair, and was instantly mortified that she had done so.

"I've called, Lady Mainthorpe, because I wish to acquaint myself further with you – and your cousin."

Hope stifled as gasp at his words.

"That is… flattering… Your Grace…"

Evelyn sounded as if she found it alarming, rather than flattering, at least to Hope's ear.

"I've just come from Chatterley, and a rather long conversation with my mother." the Duke said. He glanced at Evelyn, but his eyes immediately turned back to rest on Hope. Evelyn made a polite noise, but was clearly waiting to hear something which might make sense of him choosing to call, and without notice. "You know Lady and Lord Dunham, I believe, Lady Mainthorpe?"

"Yes, we attended their Ball but two weeks ago," Evelyn responded, a little frostily, Hope thought – perhaps Evelyn was as confused as she was, at this point, and Evelyn had never dealt well with lack of clarity.

The Duke nodded and said, "Yes. Well, Lady Dunham is a close friend of my mother." Hope was beginning to wonder what purpose the conversation served, becoming more confused by the minute. "Apparently, when last Lady Dunham called upon my mother, she spoke very highly of you, my Lady," the Duke said, inclining his head towards Evelyn. "And then, at an afternoon tea my mother held, Lady Tarrington, Lady Walsingham, and Lady Tennant all recommended Lady Hope as a most charming person."

He inclined his head to Hope.

Hope's thoughts were spinning as she tried to comprehend that a Duke was complimenting *her*. A Duke!

But Evelyn still looked as confused as Hope felt, perhaps more so.

"Lady Tarrington, Lady Walsingham and Lady Tennant?" she asked in surprise. "Yes... they have met Hope," she said slowly, raising an eyebrow. "And my cousin certainly is a charming young woman... But... I do not see, quite, Your Grace, exactly why your mother's friends' opinions of Lady Hope, however flattering, have led you to our door today...?"

Evelyn seemed unsure what to make of the Duke, and her brow crinkled in a manner that Hope knew always preceded a megrim. Hope met Evelyn's eyes, which were filled with slight concern. She knew what was going through her cousin's mind - why should an important man show favour to her? Lady Hope Spencer, a young lady of genteel obscurity with no fortune, no wealthy relations beyond Evelyn, and no useful connections, was not the sort of young woman normally sought out by a Duke. It was little wonder that her cousin should feel protective of her, since there seemed no logical explanation for the Duke's interest.

The Duke gazed at Hope for a moment, as if assessing her in some way, and a shiver ran through her. She had the oddest sense, in that moment, that he was silently begging her to understand something. But she had no idea what that something was.

"I have a very large estate," the Duke said, finally turning his gaze back to Evelyn. "And I have many tenants, all of whom trust me. I wish to never betray that trust."

He spoke with an air of explanation, but Hope had no idea what he was explaining or why.

"Of course," Evelyn said calmly, though Hope could sense her frustration at the man's apparently purposeless intrusion into their day. "And I am certain that you have a *great many things to do*." She gave him a significant look, but the Duke was gazing at Hope again. With a touch of impatience in her honey sweet voice, Evelyn said, "Isn't it kind, Hope, of the Duke to take time out of his busy day to call on us?"

Hope blushed, avoiding the Duke's eyes, a little embarrassed that Evelyn was so pointedly attempting to get him to leave. When she finally gathered the courage to look up, she noticed that the Duke was smiling at her in satisfaction. Satisfaction about what, was the important question – and being looked at like that ruffled her pride somewhat, for it was almost proprietary, and she responded in a firmer tone than she had intended.

"Yes, we so appreciate your kindness, Your Grace."

The Duke's eyebrows flew up in surprise, but he stared at Hope even more curiously.

"Indeed, I take my duties towards my neighbours as seriously as I do towards my tenants. If Lady Mainthorpe or yourself ever have the slightest need," he inclined his head, "you may call on me."

With that, he smiled for the first time, and Hope couldn't help but smile back. Even as her mind processed the fact that he must actually live close by, when in London, she was also realising that she liked the way that his eyes crinkled, and he seemed a little less intimidating for the smile, as he bid the two women farewell and thanked them for their hospitality.

When the Duke had finally left the room, Hope settled back in her chair with a smile on her face.

"Well, I never!" Evelyn fumed, crossing her arms, and looking furiously after the Duke. "No warning, no invitation, no comprehensible conversation! I cannot account for it, can you, Hope?"

Hope stirred out of her daydreaming.

"Truthfully, I cannot."

"These great men are often abrupt and eccentric," Evelyn mused, "but the Duke seems especially so." She turned curiously to her cousin. "Hope, did it not seem as though the Duke was particularly interested in you?"

"Certainly not," Hope said, looking down shyly but unable to hide her smile, and thinking that perhaps, yes, he had been.

"I see no reason why he should be," Evelyn agreed, looking disturbed. "Now, my dear, you are a wonderful girl," she said hastily, "but a Duke simply has no cause to give particular favour to a young lady of your rank or circumstances. I fear that some mischief is up. Birkchester does not have a bad reputation, so I don't know what to think – but I warn you, dear cousin, to stay away from him. Put him out of your mind, and let us treat him deferentially, but distantly, when we see him. There is no reason for him to be tied to us, nor we to him. Let us treat him with caution."

Evelyn signalled to the servant to clear away the tea tray, and beckoned Hope to the piano in the smaller parlour. Hope obediently followed, but a smile betrayed her as she sang with particular gusto, intrigued by the mysterious attentions of a wealthy and handsome man.

Chapter Four

Xavier settled back against the squabs in his carriage, dropping his hat onto the seat beside him. That had been, as a social call, a complete disaster. He had not known what to say – had found just the fact of sitting beside Lady Hope Spencer enough to befuddle his mind, and had singularly failed to achieve even moderately sensible conversation.

What was it, about this one woman, which affected him so differently from every other woman he had ever met?

He shook his head, staring out of the carriage window as it took him the short distance to Harte House. He was grateful that his mother was still at Chatterley Park – for if she had been here, she would have been enquiring, every day, about his progress in finding a woman to marry. Everything he had said to Lady Mainthorpe and Lady Hope had been true – his mother made it her business to discover everything she could about every new young woman who came out each year – she saw it as part of her duty to her son.

But, surely, now that he looked back on that excruciating call he had just finished, he should have found his own words to compliment the young woman, rather than repeating the remarks of others – however positive they may have been.

He did not know how to do this.

This 'calling upon a young lady, with the intent of probably courting her' was not something he had ever done before. He would have to try again. There was nothing else for it. Perhaps, if he regularly walked in the park in the square near both Lady Mainthorpe's house and his, he might see her, might manage to encounter her in a less formal setting?

It was as good a plan as any – and in the meantime, perhaps Smith would come back to him with more information about her family, which would allow him to get a better certainty that she was as she appeared to be. Although, he thought wryly – he was no longer sure that he cared at all about her family history – he cared about her. For she had captivated him from the start, and every time he saw her, that feeling became stronger.

✳✳✳✳✳

The next day passed uneventfully. It was a bright, sunny day, and the two cousins had been expecting to pay a few calls, but Evelyn begged off, telling Hope that they would make their social calls another day. As Hope had expected, her cousin spent the day in bed with a terrible megrim, which had developed soon after His Grace of Birkchester had left.

Evelyn was still quite upset about the Duke's unexpected visit, it seemed, and when Hope asked her why, Evelyn spoke tersely.

"For the life of me, I cannot imagine why a Duke would go out of his way to be introduced, to enquire about us from his mother's friends, and then to invite himself to tea while talking about nothing. I warn you, that man is up to some mischief. Oh, I do detest not knowing. I wish Mainthorpe was here. He'd know what to do about all of this."

As Hope carefully fixed her bonnet and drew on her gloves early that evening, she thought about how pleased she was that Lord Mainthorpe was *not* there. He would be in Hertford County, some miles away, on estate business until the end of the month, at least. Which suited Hope's plans for the evening nicely.

Evelyn was still abed, after having elected to have an early dinner in her room. She had insisted that Hope join her, which she had willingly done, although Evelyn did little but fret about the Duke. It seemed that her cousin had become more protective of Hope since the Duke's flattering attentions, but, conversely, Hope had begun to feel rather more brave and independent.

Now, as Evelyn settled towards early sleep, Hope gathered her new found courage and pulled on her favourite light-weight pelisse over her day gown, then secretly slipped out of the townhouse, carefully avoiding the servants, moving as quietly as she could.

She soothed her conscience with the knowledge that Evelyn would already be asleep; it was still early evening, quite light outside, and the park was only a step away, in the centre of the large square on which Lady Mainthorpe's townhouse stood.

A pretty glow came to her face as Hope breathed in the fresh air and gazed happily at the couples promenading around.

She had taken barely twenty steps into the park when a deep voice spoke, seeming very close to her

"I wonder if they're in love?"

She jumped and whipped around to see the Duke of Birkchester approaching her. She stopped, and waited until he stood beside her. Looking up to meet his eyes, she was struck again by how tall he was, and she felt a little tongue tied, but, after a moment of silence, she composed herself and curtsied.

"Your Grace."

He bowed in return.

"May I take a turn about the park with you, Lady Hope?"

Hope mutely put her hand on his proffered arm as they began the park's circuit. She was in shock at the turn of events, and for all of her girlish excitement over the Duke's attentions, she felt something akin to dread at meeting him at this moment, alone. Even if they were in a very public place, to meet him unchaperoned was quite improper. But... she had not meant to...

Still... Evelyn believed that he was plotting some mischief, Hope wasn't supposed to be at the park, she was alone, even if there were other people close by, and it would soon be dark. All of these things converged to form an uneasy sensation in the pit of her stomach, and she glanced up at the window she knew to be Evelyn's. If she was caught walking alone in the park with the Duke, she would surely be reprimanded severely, and perhaps even be sent home to the country.

Hope cast a surreptitious glance up at the Duke's handsome face. How had he come to be at the park just as she had arrived?

Could he have been watching the house?

What if Evelyn was right, and he was not to be trusted? Hope's imagination ran wild, and she didn't realise that the Duke was speaking to her until he stopped walking.

"I beg your pardon, I... I was woolgathering..."

She was almost stammering, as she looked at his inquisitive face.

"I was just complimenting you on your cousin's charm," he said with a smile. Although his eyes and mouth were very serious, there was something wonderful about the way they looked when he smiled. "Those of my acquaintance have only good things to say about Lady Mainthorpe and her husband."

Hope felt confused again. Although Evelyn had become comfortable in society, due to her husband's wealth and title, there was still nothing in particular to recommend her, much less Hope, to someone like a Duke. It also sounded almost as though he had been asking his friends about them. Hope felt uneasily as if some plot was thickening around her and, recalling her cousin's distrust of the Duke, she determined to have the truth out once and for all.

"Pardon my boldness, Your Grace," she said abruptly, turning her petite face up to his, "but is there some kinship you feel towards us, towards myself, and my cousin, some reason that you have lately favoured us with your presence?"

The Duke looked surprised but impressed by her frankness.

"Just so, just so. There is no better time to tell you. Lady Hope," he said, gazing into her bright green eyes with his hazel ones, "I want to get married."

"Oh. I am happy for you, Your Grace."

Hope summoned a smile and began to walk again.

"You misunderstand me," the Duke said, gently taking her hand and pulling her back. "I wish to be married to *you*."

Hope's first instinct was to laugh.

"Forgive me. I do misunderstand you," she said when she had recovered herself. "I thought that I just heard you say that you wished to marry me."

"You heard correctly," the Duke said, now taking both of her hands in his own. "Will you marry me, Lady Hope? Please say yes."

Hope disentangled her hands from his and took a step back, a new flush rising to her cheeks – one of anger. Duke or not, he had no right to tease her, especially considering the disparity in their rank and their lack of familiarity. He could not, in any possible way, be serious. And knowing that her mother's finances and survival depended on her making a good match, to be teased on such a matter tore at her quite cruelly.

"Your Grace, I barely know you. I cannot countenance the idea that you are serious," she said, her voice shaking, wishing that she had the right to ask him forthrightly, 'are you quite mad?' She forced a smile and said lightly, "Why, I really should not even be walking with you tonight, much less marrying you. I pray you forgive me - I must get back to the house."

She had turned away, and begun to stride back towards the townhouse when the Duke called after her.

"Wait!" He quickly caught up and said, with a contrite expression, "Forgive me. I have made an utter mess of this, I'm afraid." Hope waited for an explanation, unsure exactly what he meant, and feeling even more desperate to escape him. "How do I say this?" the Duke hesitated. "I am the master of a very large estate and its tenants," he started.

"Yes, you mentioned that."

Hope continued to look at him expectantly, feeling annoyed again.

"Well, I will try to explain," the Duke said, now speaking more quickly. "My tenants are disquieted, and my mother worries."

"Because...?"

"Because my family has owned Chatterley for three hundred years," he said bluntly, twisting his hat nervously in his hands. "And if I die without an heir... it may not be imminent, for I am in good health, but still..."

"You... want to marry me... because you want an heir?" Hope said slowly, watching the Duke's face.

He looked relieved and said, "Just so."

Hope ignored the slight sting which came with realising that she was not wanted for her personality, or even for her appearance, but forced herself to focus on the heart of the matter. She forced a laugh and spoke lightly.

"Why, there's no shame in that. There are many fine ladies who will make you a good match – a far better match than I would make you." She shifted uncomfortably and made to leave again. "But you don't need my help in selecting a wife. I would know little about the process anyway."

"Wait – please," the Duke begged her. "You don't understand, I have thought about this for some time."

He sighed and gazed at her.

Hope waited, uncertain again, and rather shocked at all that had just occurred – he could not be serious!

"What don't I understand, Your Grace?"

"Too often I have been sought out as a match for my money, my title. Young women flock around me – but none of them see me, they only see the chance to be a Duchess, to be important, or to have wealth greater than they have now. I want a quiet life, a peaceful home with little fuss, that's all. I don't need any more money or power – I have quite enough; the woman who would normally marry a man in my position is not the woman I am looking for." He stepped closer and said persuasively, "The first time I saw you, I had the feeling that you were somewhat of a kindred spirit, that you would have preferred the quiet of the country to the glitter of the ballroom. Will you say yes?"

Hope reluctantly shook the cobwebs from her head.

"I am sorry," she firmly apologised, "but I cannot."

She could not, because she could not believe that he meant it. It felt like a trap, like a ploy to lead her on, and then leave her with nothing. Perhaps it was just Evelyn's uncertainty infecting her too, but she could not imagine that he meant it, no matter how sincere he sounded. Even if he did mean it, she would want more time to get to know him first, to be sure that she could bear to live with him, for the rest of her life.

But... what about Mother? Surely, a Duke is the best possible match you could make?

The thought slipped through her mind, and she pushed it aside. Despite her mother's ill health, and their precarious financial position, she must be sensible, must be certain that the man she married would actually help her mother... before she committed to marriage. And she knew almost nothing about Birkchester, beyond the fact that he confused her, every time they met.

He looked at her, and something passed across his expression, of almost sadness, and almost desperation. She ignored it, curtsied, and rapidly walked to back to the townhouse. Darkness was just beginning to fall as Hope opened the front door. She looked behind her, but the Duke had not followed, and she breathed a sigh of relief.

Amazingly, no one seemed to have realised her absence. She removed her hat and gloves and crept upstairs, slipping into bed just as a maid arrived to check that nothing more was needed, before seeking her own bed. Hope lay awake for hours, tossing and turning and staring at the silvering of moonlight which filtered into the room.

*****

Why had he been so foolish as to ask her, without preamble, in the middle of a park?

Xavier shook his head sadly, watching as she walked away.

He should have expected the response he had received – why would a young lady believe him sincere, when he had caught her by surprise?

Nonetheless, he was determined to try again – for her reaction, just now, had shown him, yet again, that she was different. He could not imagine any other of the young ladies of the *ton* refusing an offer of marriage from him, no matter how badly presented it was. Lady Hope seemed to have no greed in her, no manipulation or deceit – which reinforced his belief that they would suit each other, that they would be able to live peacefully with each other.

He would summon Mr Smith tomorrow, to hear what the man had discovered about her family – whether he would then allow that information, whatever it was, to affect his feelings, he did not know.

Chapter Five

The next morning, Hope awoke feeling discontented and unrested. All night she had alternated between 'It didn't really happen, did it?' and 'You should have accepted, you fool!'.

She still didn't quite know *how* the events of the night before could have taken place, and she knew that no one would believe her if she did tell of them– especially since the Duke might very well deny his part, given that his marriage proposal had been declined.

So Hope said nothing as she sat at the breakfast table with Evelyn, who was apparently over her megrim.

"I'm not going to worry about the Duke problem," Evelyn said briskly as she dug into a poached egg. "I have decided that his attentions were just the passing fancy of a wealthy eccentric, and it means nothing for us." Hope held back a yawn and put her head down on the table. "My dear, you look unwell," Evelyn commented in concern.

"No, no, I'm just... tired," Hope said, trying to smile.

"Well, I'm glad to hear it, although you should take some rest during the day - there is another Ball tonight at Lord Forth's, do you remember?"

Hope repressed a groan of dread.

"I do hope that we don't see the Duke."

"Let us avoid him" Evelyn agreed, nodding sagely.

"For Lady Hope."

The butler entered the breakfast room and proffered a letter on the correspondence tray.

"Who is it from?" Evelyn asked as Hope quickly broke the seal and scanned the letter. "My dear, what is it?"

Hope felt the shock overcome her, and she was sure that her face turned white as she slumped back in her chair, for Evelyn looked very concerned, and beckoned a servant over to refill Hope's teacup. Hope allowed the letter to fall to the table, releasing it as if it was a poisonous insect. Evelyn reached out and took Hope's hand.

Hope took a rather large mouthful of the tea.

"I *must* go home."

"Now, just catch your breath for a moment," Evelyn soothed her, patting her comfortingly on the arm. "Why do you have to go home?"

Hope mutely handed her the letter and Evelyn's face turned solemn as she read it. "...'The Creditors took everything... fine china sold... nothing left but my bed, a wicker chair and some plates... love, Mother.' Oh Hope, I am *so* sorry - I had no idea it was this bad. Otherwise, I would not have permitted my aunt to manage your home alone."

"Nor I," Hope said, putting an icy cold hand to her hot forehead. "I suppose my mother hid the true state of our finances from me. I thought that I knew, and certainly, I knew that it was not good… but this… I suppose that she wanted to make sure that I came to London. But I *must* go home!"

"My aunt *did* want you to come to London," Evelyn countered gently, looking at the letter again. "She says that she does not feel much worse, and that she has resolved to buy back the china when she can. Don't panic, dear, your mother sounds safe and sound. It is unfortunate that you have lost so much of the furnishings, but she does imply that the creditors having taken all of that will at least delay any further demands. I will see if I can convince her to allow me to support her with some funds for immediate expenses – and we will arrange at least the minimum of furniture." Hope nodded obediently, brushing away her tears, and Evelyn said "Good girl. Now, go and select your outfit for the Ball tonight – this will all be solved when we find you a good husband!"

Evelyn smiled fondly at her cousin, not knowing the additional anguish she had just heaped upon her.

Hope sought refuge in her room, pondering with dread what she had done by turning down a Duke. What did it matter if he was slightly mad and had picked her to marry in a fit of rebellious fancy? She and her mother might be on the streets if she didn't marry soon.

A Duke! If Hope married a Duke, she would have a beautiful home, a title, and the ability to provide for her mother and save them both from destitution. What was love, in the face of the need for security?

She allowed her tears of regret to fall.

It was an odd moment – she felt grief for the love she would likely never have, if she married simply to solve their financial problems, but she also cried because she felt a fool to have rejected the Duke in the first place.

Of course, the Duke would most likely want nothing to do with her now.

Almost certainly, she had ruined the best chance of improving her life that she had ever had. How she dreaded going to the Ball and possibly encountering the Duke.

What had she done?

****

That night, Hope dreaded leaving the carriage as it pulled up in front of Lord Forth's townhouse.

"Now, don't worry," Evelyn said kindly. "I'm sure that your mother is fine. We'll just greet the host and hostess, circulate a little, then leave early if you like. You need not dance unless you want to."

Hope nodded mutely and took a deep breath, trying to assure herself that if the Duke was at the Ball, he would certainly avoid her – it was impossible that he would want to publicise his marriage proposal to her. Armed with this certainty, Hope walked into the ballroom, half trying to hide behind Evelyn.

"Lady Hope!"

Almost immediately, a flock of chattering young ladies descended upon a bewildered Hope.

No one had wanted to talk to her the last Ball, yet it seemed that, now, she was the most popular woman at this Ball. After she recovered from her surprise, Hope began to enjoy herself. Evelyn hovered at her elbow, looking gratified at her cousin's popularity, but clearly wondering why it had occurred.

It wasn't until a few hours into the night that the reason for Hope's newfound friends was revealed.

"So how do you come to know the Duke?" one particularly over cheerful woman said with a sly smile.

"W-what?"

Hope stuttered in shock, suddenly fearing that her secret was about to be revealed.

"Don't be so coy! He was at Lady Ward's afternoon musicale, and we all overheard him talking to her! Birkchester sounded quite interested in you, and he had only good things to say," the woman continued with a sly smile. "There must be some story to it. No man speaks like that of a woman unless he has at least some small interest in her."

There was a long pause as all of the women around her stared hopefully, and suddenly Hope realised why they were surrounding her, what they wanted. They wanted to know if Birkchester might marry her, or if not, if she might help them closer to him, themselves. She glanced at Evelyn, who only batted her fan as though to say 'Say what you like'.

Hope opened her mouth hesitantly. If she told only the extent of what her cousin knew – that the Duke had spoken to them but three times, and that they knew little about him – all of her newfound friends would quickly disperse. But if she told the truth, that the Duke had proposed to her... well, she wasn't about to do that.

"Lady Hope?" A deep voice solved her problem. Hope turned and saw the Duke of Birkchester standing behind her, smiling. Something like fear, mingled with anticipation, filled her heart and she swallowed nervously. She had been wondering if the Duke would ignore her, and thereby change the attitudes of her fickle new friends, or even reveal his denied proposal in anger, thus exposing her as a fool. Strangely enough, he seemed to be considering neither of these choices. On the contrary, he appeared quite amiable as he bowed to her and smiled. "May I have the honour of the next dance, Lady Hope?"

The women around her twittered and giggled excitedly, while at her side Evelyn looked thundery. Hope could sense that her cousin was on the verge of bursting out, 'May I ask just what your intentions are towards my cousin, Your Grace?' and was barely restraining herself.

To forestall this embarrassing situation and to prevent the secret of the Duke's proposal from being revealed, Hope ignored her cousin's knit brows.

"Of course, Your Grace."

Just then the music for the next set began, and Hope glided away on the Duke's arm.

A rush of varying emotions assailed her as she avoided the Duke's eyes during the stately minuet. She didn't quite know how to act, because she was more and more certain that she had been too hasty in turning him down. But... how did you explain to a gentleman that, upon reflection, you would like to change the answer you had given him?

The letter from her mother about the creditors had put things into perspective and Hope now realised how absurd it was for her to reject a marriage proposal from a wealthy titled man.

Of course, she didn't know anything about him - he might well be silly, cruel, or unintelligent – although nothing she had seen of him so far suggested that. He was, perhaps, a little eccentric, but did not seem in any way unkind – quite the opposite. She reminded herself that any man with wealth and a title might be cruel, or unreasonable - and she must marry a man with a fortune soon, or risk worse than dealing with a silly or unjust husband.

Hope made up her mind to reverse her mistake, to convince the Duke, somehow, to ask her again, no matter what it took to do that. Just *how* to go about it was the question.

The Duke looked relaxed and comfortable, as though the events in the park the night before hadn't happened at all. Hope was entirely too shy to broach the delicate subject, so she tried to behave as if she had not a concern in the world.

Now that she had made a conscious decision to 'catch' the Duke, however, the fear of having already irrevocably deflected his attentions haunted her, and made her ill at ease. She grew nervous as the set ended and the Duke bowed to her, afraid that her slim chance of re-earning his regard had disappeared. Having steeled herself to be simply delivered back to Evelyn, and left, she breathed easier as he held out an arm and asked if she'd like to take a turn about the room.

"Yes. Yes, I would like that."

Hope was ashamed to note that she was almost gushing at the man in her enthusiasm. But the Duke just smiled and they began a slow promenade about the perimeter of the room. The silence between them would have been companionable, had Hope not been so nervous.

Finally, the Duke spoke.

"I... may I beg your forgiveness for my behaviour in the park, Lady Hope? It was absolutely unforgivable."

Hope had not expected that at all, and hid a relieved smile behind her fluttering fan.

"Your Grace, you are forgiven."

"Thank you."

There was a pause as Hope glanced at the Duke, wondering what she should say to establish her newfound interest in him. She had never been good at flirting, and she felt quite out of her depth. The Duke had proposed to her, but they were not yet familiar with each other, and he was her superior in social rank.

"Will... you be in London long?" Hope asked hesitantly.

The Duke shook his head.

"No, I'm off soon to stay with my friend, Lord Ashton, at his estate."

"Oh."

Hope's face fell and she desperately considered what possibly way she might get him to propose again, before he left. She said nothing, however, and seeing her downcast face the Duke smiled.

"If you wish me to leave sooner, I certainly will respect your wishes."

"No!" Hope exclaimed a little too forcefully. She bit her lip and amended, "I did not mean to imply that I hoped you would leave sooner – far from it! I too have regrets about my actions last night. I hope that we can get to know each other a little better before you leave London."

The Duke looked surprised but pleased.

"If you feel that such a meeting would be agreeable with you, might I call at a time of your choosing?"

Hope thought quickly. Evelyn would certainly wish to ask the Duke a multitude of questions about his intentions, if he called on them, which would most likely cause him to deny any interest in Hope before she'd had a chance to set things right. No, it was much safer to meet him on her own and extract a second proposal - even if the very thought of going so far outside the bounds of propriety was deeply shocking. Hope had always been well behaved – that she now considered meeting a gentleman, alone, startled even her.

"Perhaps – perhaps we could meet tomorrow in the park... in the early afternoon?"

Hope spoke quickly, waiting with bated breath for his answer. She was afraid that she had appeared unladylike in her proposal, knowing full well that it was, by many people's judgement, completely inappropriate, even if there would be other people about. But the Duke did not seem concerned, and only bowed as they reached Evelyn and murmured, "Of course, if I must wait all day, I will be there."

Those words left her feeling unaccountably warm, and a little flustered, but she smiled, and thanked him for the dance, before watching as he moved away from them. As soon as he was some distance away, all of the young women who had been thronged around her before returned, eager to question her, but she demurely deflected their questions and ended the night as quite the popular young lady.

She suspected that they all hoped to be close if the Duke lost interest in Hope, so that he might notice them instead, but Hope had the strangest feeling that the Duke would not care for any of them.

Evelyn, however, was not impressed, and Hope rather dreaded her cousin's impending lecture as she stepped into the carriage at the end of the night. Never had Hope felt more like a rebellious child being scolded by her elders. But ironically, Hope was trying to do the mature thing and secure a future for herself and her mother. Why couldn't her cousin understand?

"Did you enjoy yourself, my dear?" Evelyn asked as they began rumbling back home.

"Indeed, it was most pleasant," Hope said nonchalantly, trying not to sound excited. She knew what was coming next as her cousin opened her mouth again, so she hurriedly said, "the Duke is quite agreeable, is he not?"

Evelyn sighed and folded her hands in her lap.

"I dare say he is, Hope. But my dear, you mustn't give him the wrong idea."

"The wrong idea?" Hope asked, starting to feel like the victim of misplaced judgement. "Is it wrong that he is paying his attentions to me?"

"Now, don't get angry, my dear girl, or take this the wrong way." Evelyn seemed to steel herself to deliver a lecture she had been wanting to deliver for some time. "A Duke – doesn't – pay the type of attention he has been showering upon us unless he wants something in return." Hope stared outside at the gas lit streets and felt as if her night had been spoiled. "You can offer him neither wealth nor connections, through no fault of your own. So what else might he be looking for?"

"My birth is not so low as that!" Hope exclaimed indignantly, wiping away a single tear. "And I am sure that the Duke is not that kind of a man. I cannot imagine him seeking to take advantage of me, in any way!"

"We don't *know* him, though," Evelyn said, and Hope realised how concerned her cousin truly was.

"What if – what if – he wanted to marry me?"

Hope quickly looked down, afraid to see her cousin's face. But she needn't have feared. Evelyn shook her head and spoke rather dourly.

"Let's not hold out hope for that, my dear, just because he has been polite to you. He's a Duke – he can have his pick of any young woman – and most have far better connections than you have, and far larger dowries."

Hope considered trying to convince her cousin that she had been proposed to; but what if the Duke didn't propose a second time? If that was the case, then all she would do by mentioning it to Evelyn was embarrass herself. And even if she might be able to manage to convince her cousin that the Duke had proposed, Evelyn seemed so prejudiced against the idea that Hope didn't want to expend the energy in arguing, so she stayed silent.

But she resolved to somehow get a renewed proposal from the Duke the next day, no matter what.

*****

Xavier spent the rest of the Ball feeling rather pleased with himself. This time, he had managed to speak with her, to dance with her, without causing her distress or confusion. And she had agreed to meet him again. Her request to meet in the park near their homes was a little unusual, but he suspected that she felt that both of them were more likely to converse if not directly under the eye of her dragon of a protective cousin.

He could not fault Lady Mainthorpe for her care of her charge, but it did disturb him that he seemed to, somehow, have made a less than desirable impression on the lady. He would simply have to prove himself to be of genuine intent.

He was not going to give up – Lady Hope Spencer fascinated him, and every time he saw her, she seemed even more suited to be his wife. Perhaps, tomorrow, depending on how their conversation went, he might ask her again? Perhaps, this time, he might get it right?

Could he hope that she would accept? Or was he rushing things far too much?

Chapter Six

Mr Smith set a pile of papers down upon Xavier's desk, then took the seat which Xavier had waved him to.

"Your Grace, your instincts were very much correct with respect to those investments. I don't have all of the details as yet, but what I do have does not look good. I will wait to bring things to you until I have the last of the information – but I am already drawing up a plan for you to cut off those associations, as soon as we are sure."

"Very good, Smith. But… about the other matter I asked you to look into…?"

"Lady Hope Spencer, Your Grace?"

"Yes."

Smith fidgeted a little, sifting through his papers, then opened a folder and studied what was in it. Xavier frowned – the man was making a drama about it, instead of simply speaking.

"Your Grace, the family is an old one – her father, now deceased, was the Earl of Salenton. It has never been a wealthy Earldom, and her mother was only the daughter of a Baron – she did not bring much of a dowry to the match. The current Earl is a third cousin, as Lady Hope has no siblings, and I believe that she, and her mother, have a single small property – everything else went to the cousin with the title. There was some small degree of scandal whispered about the father's death, however it was well hushed up. He was a gambler, and late in his life, somewhat of a drunkard, I believe. He likely left them more in the way of debts than funds, though I've not uncovered any specific details to confirm that."

"I see. So, Lady Hope is probably in somewhat straightened circumstances, but is otherwise completely respectable?"

"I would call that an accurate assessment, Your Grace. I am still enquiring, politely, in an attempt to uncover whether there is any remaining debt or problem – but even if there is, the Lady can only be blameless in the matter."

"Thank you. Let me know when you have any further information on either matter."

Smith gathered his papers, and rose, bowing.

"Of course, your Grace."

He took himself off, and Xavier sat, staring out of his study window, at the park where, in a few hours' time, he would meet Lady Hope Spencer, again. He was cautiously pleased with what Smith had discovered – but also puzzled. If Lady Hope was in straightened circumstances, then she was even more intriguing than before – for he would have expected a young woman with an impoverished family to eagerly seek the chance to marry a man like himself.

Could it be that she was genuinely more focussed on the person, than their wealth or position, despite her own family's need?

That seemed extraordinary, yet everything he had seen of her indicated it to be truth. Which only made him want to marry her more. Made him, in fact, care for her more, not just as a solution to his problem, although he was chagrined to admit that it had certainly begun that way, but as a person.

If Smith did uncover any more debt hanging over the family, that was something which he could easily address, if he married her – and he would willingly do, if for no other reason than that she had not attempted to manipulate him to that end.

✱✱✱✱✱

As soon as she woke on the morning after the Ball, Hope remembered the commitment she had made the previous evening.

She was to meet the Duke, in the park, in the early afternoon. Just the thought of it made her heart pound, and her mouth go dry. That was, she assured herself, only because she was about to do something outside the bounds of propriety – not at all because she was excited by the idea of seeing the Duke again…

But she needed a way to ensure that she could meet him, without Evelyn knowing. A way that she, as yet, had not the slightest idea of. As Charlotte, her maid, walked in to empty the chamber pot, and ask if Hope was ready to rise, an idea sprang into her mind.

She started coughing and sneezing violently, praying that the maid would be convinced by her performance.

"Oh, my Lady! Are you all right?"

Charlotte hurried over in concern.

Hope moaned and tossed in response, and Charlotte left and quickly returned with Evelyn, who was half dressed, a wrap thrown around her.

"Hope! Whatever is the matter?" her cousin exclaimed in distress. "Are you ill?"

Hope looked pitiful and nodded.

"Oh dear, it must have been the rain earlier this week, and you going about without your wrap," Evelyn scolded. She sighed. "And we were going to make our afternoon calls today. Well, we can go tomorrow."

"No!" Hope exclaimed, sitting up in bed. She quickly lay back down and made her voice sound weak again. "I couldn't hold you back from making your social calls. Please, go on without me."

Evelyn looked at her dubiously.

"Are you sure? We can go tomorrow."

"Really," Hope smiled weakly. "I don't think that I'll be fit to go anywhere for some days."

Evelyn hesitated, but finally nodded.

"I'll leave Charlotte here with you this afternoon, and I'll only be gone for an hour or two. Are you quite sure that you'll be all right if I leave?"

Hope nodded. Evelyn accepted that, and went to finish dressing.

After Hope had eaten breakfast in bed, Evelyn came up to chat with her and read a little from a book of poems. It was obvious that she felt badly about her words of the night before, when she had been so dismissive of the very idea that a Duke would be interested in Hope. Whilst Hope appreciated her conciliatory gesture, she kept glancing at the clock on the mantel, growing nervous that the Duke would be gone by the time she escaped to the park. It was two hours past noon when Evelyn finally took her leave to go out on her planned calls, telling Hope to rest well while she was gone.

For those two hours, Hope had been yawning, and making certain that she looked tired, and listless. Now, as soon as she heard the front door close, she yawned loudly and turned sleepily to Charlotte.

"Please, may I be alone? I'm very tired and I need to be completely alone to sleep."

"But your cousin –"

"I'm a very light sleeper when I am not well," Hope added emphatically. "Please don't disturb me until my cousin returns."

Charlotte curtseyed and left the room, shaking her head a little in worry, but unwilling to argue further with a Lady. Hope smiled. Her plan had worked – so far.

She slipped out of bed and stuffed some extra blankets into a person-shaped lump under the covers, then put her ear to the bedroom door. Hearing nothing, she quickly dressed in a simple day gown, and slipped out into the hall. She had watched the movements of the servants often enough to know that at this time of day, there would be few about – the morning cleaning was all done, and the preparations for dinner were not yet happening.

She watched from the landing until the footman on duty had left the front hall for a moment, then stole quietly out of the front door and almost ran to the park. She was terrified that the Duke would have left, despite what he had said about waiting all day, it being some hours past when she had said that she would meet him.

But she needn't have worried. As she hurried into the Park, feeling grateful that no one else was about to see her, the Duke rose from his seat on a sheltered bench in one of the clusters of trees.

"Lady Hope," he murmured, taking her hand, and kissing it.

Hope blushed, touched that he still wanted to see her after her rejection of his marriage proposal. She also discovered that she was truly happy to see him, her heart beating a little faster as he pressed his lips to her hand.

"Your Grace…"

"Shall we walk a little?"

He offered his arm, and she placed her hand on it, conscious as she did of the warmth of it, the sheer strength of the man. He was so tall that she felt quite small beside him. Again, she thought how handsome he looked, and how kind his expression was. Hope wondered, now that she looked at him, and simply took in the man, without letting social judgements or Evelyn's opinion get in the way, what exactly was *stopping* her from marrying the Duke.

Of a certainty, she didn't 'know' him, but who did really know their spouse before marriage? Most girls she knew of married for money, family advantage, or convenience. She had heard of bad matches made, both for advantage, and for love, but those which went bad were certainly few and far between.

Perhaps she was naïve, and the bad ones were simply not talked about… but still.

In this case, she was discovering that she truly liked what she knew of the Duke so far. Perhaps more than liked. Could she possibly be falling in love with the Duke? It would certainly make everything easier. She had planned on marrying him for his money – for the sake of her mother, planned on being just like all of those young women she – and he, if what he had said was true – despised, and seeking only advantage - but as they walked together something was rapidly changing in her heart. She no longer saw him as just a necessity to be tolerated, for the sake of saving her mother. He had become something more.

The very first time she had seen him, he had intrigued her – for his response to the incident with the wine had not been what she expected – and, ever since, he had surprised her – admittedly, he had confused her too, but in the end, she had moved past that. Then, when he had agreed to her rather improper request to meet her here, and had, instead of berating her for the manner in which she had refused his proposal, actually apologised, she had felt her heart swell with a care for him which had not been there before.

When he had first asked her to marry him, here in this very park, he had claimed to want to marry her solely for the more tender and touching sentiments of, if not love, then kinship of souls, and comfort.

It had seemed absolutely incredible that she should be the chosen object of his affections – she, who was a little awkward, quite shy, with a family in reduced circumstances and a life which, without a good marriage, was destined for sad obscurity.

Hadn't he said that he longed for the same future as she?

Not riches or Balls or notoriety, but a peaceful, quiet home in the countryside.

How were they *not* right for each other?

All of this was going through Hope's mind as they walked through the Park, talking about insignificant things. She was so happy just being in his presence – and his willingness to treat her with decency and friendship betrayed his true, gentlemanly nature.

She suddenly stopped in the middle of her sentence, and the Duke met her gaze. She stood silently as he smiled, then spoke, apparently unconcerned by her abrupt interruption of their discussion of the appeal of formal gardens.

"What is it, Hope?" The name slipped out from his mouth and he immediately looked filled with uncertainty. "I beg your pardon," he said, giving a deep bow and looking stricken. "Please forgive my forwardness in using your forename."

Hope seized his hands and he looked shocked at her impropriety, but she didn't care. She had stopped speaking because she had suddenly been struck with terror at the thought of being left in London, with only Evelyn, without friendship or camaraderie, when the Duke went to his country estate or to visit his friend, as he had said he would, soon.

Why should he leave? Why should they not be together?

"Why should we not be together?"

The words were out of her mouth before she had any chance to stop them, baldly enunciating the question which had worried at her from the moment that she had stepped into the park.

The Duke looked like he couldn't believe his ears.

"I could scarcely dream of such an honour," he started with a catch in his voice. "After my insensitive blunder the other day, I could hardly expect you to wish to associate with me. I am most grateful that you granted me this meeting today – and if you truly wish for more, that is wonderful."

"I wish to see you for the rest of my days," Hope said, tears filling her large green eyes.

"Please – wait." The Duke got down on one knee and said, "If I'm allowed to dream, I must ask you, formally - my Hope – will you marry me?"

"If *I* am allowed to dream – I will accept you, heartily and happily." The Duke kissed her hands over and over as he rose and they sat on a nearby bench, sheltered from all eyes by the trees and bushes around them. "For this must be a dream, because I cannot comprehend that a man like you would want me."

Hope rested her head on the Duke's shoulder, and he slipped his arm around her.

"For the first time in my life, I saw true beauty, innocence, a pure soul in you – all of the qualities I long to spend a lifetime with. You were the first woman who never once tried to flirt with me. If I may say so, my love, you have very little guile."

Hope laughed ruefully and nodded in agreement, even though a ripple of guilt slipped through her thoughts – for she had approached this with guile, had, until even yesterday, intended to capture his attentions not because of love, but because she needed to marry well. The fact that her reasons for wishing to marry him had changed did not remove the guilt that they had been different to start with. Still, in the main, he was right – she was not a person who had ever been very good at dissembling.

"I know, Your Grace."

"Please… please say my name - Xavier," the Duke insisted, holding her hands.

"I know, Xavier," Hope amended softly.

It sent a little shiver through her, to speak to him so intimately.

The Duke looked into the distance, a hazy look in his eye.

"When you turned me down, it proved what I suspected - that you would be the first woman to not wish to marry me purely for my money and title. You are a lady of integrity, and I love you for it."

As Xavier kissed her hands again, Hope's smile faded and her stomach twisted uncomfortably, the guilt rising again – after all, she *had* decided to marry the Duke for his money. She, and her mother, needed money, and badly. But she brushed the guilt away firmly. Her feelings had changed, money wasn't the only reason she was marrying him. She was only now realising her love for Xavier - but that didn't make her love any less real because her heart had lagged a little behind her head.

As Xavier looked up, she smiled and he looked as utterly contented as she felt. They walked together back towards Evelyn's townhouse, and Hope's chest tightened in nervousness as she saw Evelyn walking up to the front door, just returning from her calls.

"I'd better hurry back before my cousin realises that I'm gone," Hope told the Duke, reluctantly beginning to remove her hand from his.

"Wait," he said, catching hold of her hand again. "Let me speak to your cousin, Hope."

"I don't know if you should, yet," she said dubiously, stealing a look at the door which had closed after Evelyn. At any moment her cousin would be discovering her deception. "I don't know if she will believe us. This will seem very sudden, and rather unlikely to her."

The Duke pulled her hand to his heart and smiled comfortingly.

"Do let me speak to her. I wish there to be no doubt about my feelings for you, and my intentions."

Xavier had spent the time waiting for Lady Hope to appear, thinking. The bench was a peaceful spot, especially at that time of day, when most of the local residents were out, making their social calls. As the time extended, he began to worry – had she meant it? Would she come? Or was he to be left here, waiting until night fell?

When she had suggested the meeting, he had felt happier than he had for quite some time, certain that, this time, now that he would have another chance to ask her, he would manage to get it right, to convince her that he meant it, that he wanted to marry her – for he did, very much.

His fears eased enormously when she did make her appearance, and he gathered his courage about him as they walked through the park, speaking of gardens, and country estates, rather than society and its gossip. The conversation was refreshing, and utterly relaxing, until she stopped both walking and talking, suddenly.

Carefully, he held himself calm, and asked her what troubled her – asked her, all without thinking, by calling her by her forename, unadorned with any title. A moment of terror caught him – would she be offended? But she was not – instead, she barely registered his apology, and then turned his world upside down with one simple question.

"Why should we not be together?"

What followed seemed still a blur, still improbable, even if wonderful, even as he walked beside her, up the steps of Lady Mainthorpe's townhouse. She had said yes! When he had asked again, she had agreed to marry him!

Now, all he had to do was convince her protectively dragonish cousin that he was completely serious in his intention to marry her. A betrothal announcement should be made as soon as possible, for he wished to marry her without delay, so that they might, together, get on with living the life they wished, and escape the grind of London society.

Chapter Seven

Hope sighed and tried to calm her nerves.

"All right. But let's hurry!"

They walked up to the door and Hope rapped the knocker. They separated as the butler opened the door and Charlotte, who was standing in the foyer, speaking with the footman, turned to her with a look of relief on her face.

"Oh, Lady Hope! I am so glad to see you safe and sound."

"Yes, Charlotte," Hope said with a smile. "I'm sorry for deceiving you, but..."

"I have something very important to discuss with Lady Mainthorpe," the Duke broke in with his deep, rich voice.

Charlotte's eyes grew wide and she quickly ushered them into the parlour, where she told them that she would send for tea, and also let Lady Mainthorpe know of the Duke's presence. Hope sat, and the Duke settled onto the couch beside her. His presence so near calmed her fears a little.

"There is no need to inform me, Charlotte, for I am here – I heard the door open, and did not stay upstairs."

Evelyn, swept into the room, removing her hat and gloves, which she handed off to Charlotte. Hope's heart filled with guilt, for she assumed that perhaps her cousin had been about to go looking for her, but had heard her voice in the hall. Hope rose and tried to speak, but Evelyn gave her a strained smile and said, "I will see His Grace alone."

Hope blushed, feeling annoyed that Evelyn felt it right to exclude her from a discussion of her own future, and bit her lip. Xavier smiled encouragingly at her and she reluctantly nodded and went upstairs to her room.

She wanted to linger outside the parlour, but she so dreaded a bad outcome of the meeting that she couldn't bear to be near. As she paced her bedroom, however, her curiosity got the better of her and she went to stand quietly on the landing, watching the closed door below, straining to hear any hint of raised voices. There was nothing but a low hum, however, and she grew worried as thirty minutes turned into an hour.

What could Evelyn and Xavier be speaking of, which took so very long?

*****

As the door closed behind Lady Hope, Xavier stood, still where he had risen as Lady Mainthorpe entered. The silence extended, as Lady Mainthorpe considered him, her expression rather thunderous. He felt rather like a schoolboy, caught out in an unapproved adventure.

After an interminable number of minutes, the lady came forward, and settled into an armchair.

"Please, be seated again, Your Grace. I presume that you have an explanation for me?"

Xavier swallowed, uncertain how best to proceed, and then decided that the simplest approach was likely to get to the heart of the matter immediately.

"Lady Mainthorpe, I have asked Lady Hope to marry me, and she has accepted. That is the thing of greatest import."

Lady Mainthorpe paled, her expression shifting from barely contained ire to shock.

"Marry you?"

"Yes, Lady Mainthorpe, I wish to marry Lady Hope."

"This is… most unexpected…"

"Lady Mainthorpe, I have long sought a young woman who might suit me – for I prefer a quiet life, mostly in the country, and want a wife who might be happy to share that, to be a comfortable companion, as well as simply fulfilling my need for an heir. I had despaired of finding a suitable young lady, until I met Lady Hope."

"But… as a Duke, forgive me for putting it so bluntly, you might choose any woman you want, and have them be grateful to marry you – why would you choose Lady Hope, who, whilst pretty, is no great beauty, and whose dowry is minimal? Admittedly, she is of good birth, but the family have never been very wealthy. It seems most irregular to me."

Well, Xavier thought, at least she was not excoriating him for the fact that Lady Hope had been out in the park with him, alone.

"Unusual or not, Lady Mainthorpe, she is my choice. Her dowry is of no consequence, for I have wealth enough, and I prefer her kind of quiet beauty of character to the rather excessive and cold beauty of many young women. Lady Hope is warm and genuine – many of the other young women might as well be marble statues."

"I see. Putting that aside for a moment, I must ask you where you had been, just before stepping into the house today – for it is obvious to me that Hope was with you, and not here, where I had thought her to be."

Ah, so he was not to escape inquisition on that matter.

"I ah... I met her in the park in the square."

"And why would you do such an improper thing, rather than call upon her here?"

Xavier drew a deep breath, searching for the right words.

"I did so because she requested it – when we danced last night, I asked to call, but she requested the park. I ah... I suspect that she wanted a chance to speak with me, before..."

He tailed off, unable to politely phrase it. To his surprise, Lady Mainthorpe laughed.

"...before I launched myself into a detailed inquiry into your intentions towards her?"

"Ah... err... just so, I believe."

"I cannot blame her, I suppose. I will admit to you that I have doubted your intentions from the start – it is unusual for a Duke to bother with a young lady who is not exceptionally beautiful, wealthy, or well connected. I still can hardly credit it."

"I assure you, I am in earnest. I want to marry her, and soon."

Lady Mainthorpe regarded him in silence for some time, and he felt himself rather rattled by that stern regard.

Nonetheless, he held steady, and simply waited.

"If you say it is so, then I must believe you, Your Grace. But please, tell me of your plans – when would you have the wedding? Will your family approve? Where will you choose to live, once married? I would not have her cut off from her mother."

Xavier allowed relief to fill him. This part, he was prepared for. They settled into a discussion during which he detailed the extent of his estates, remarked upon his widely varied investments, and spoke of Chatterley Park, the country estate where he had grown up, and planned to spend most of his time.

They also spoke of his hope that the banns might be read as soon as possible, that they might marry in but four weeks' time.

At the mention of such speed, Lady Mainthorpe questioned him closely on his expectations for how the wedding would be celebrated, and he rather thought that she feared the work which might be involved if he wanted an opulent affair.

"As far as the wedding, Lady Mainthorpe, I will leave that to you, Lady Hope's mother, and my mother to arrange between you. I trust that meets with your approval?"

"It does."

They spoke a little longer, and Lady Mainthorpe asked that he allow her the rest of the day to speak to Lady Hope, and begin the wedding planning, but that he call in two days' time, so that a more formal courtship time might proceed, even whilst the betrothal was announced and the banns read. He was disappointed by this request, but acquiesced.

Xavier asked for pen and paper, then wrote a note to Lady Hope, informing her of his intent to call, and reassuring her of his affections, before bidding Lady Mainthorpe farewell.

*****

Eventually the parlour door opened and the Duke was ushered out. Hope hurried back into her room and shut the door, heart pounding.

Would Evelyn come to tell her what they had discussed? Whatever would her cousin say, if she did?

A few minutes later, Hope heard Evelyn's footsteps outside her door, and a quiet knock came.

"Come in," Hope squeaked, perching nervously on the edge of her bed. Evelyn came in, and one look at her kind face assuaged the worst of Hope's fears. "I'm sorry—" Hope started, but Evelyn waved her apology away.

"No, dear, don't apologise." She sat down on the edge of Hope's bed and took her hand. "This is all utterly unexpected, but I cannot say that I'm displeased." Hope laughed in relief and Evelyn joined her. "In fact, I should apologise to you for dismissing you outright, when you asked *what if he wanted to marry me?* I know I was suspicious of the Duke's motives before. But he has defended himself wonderfully and put my mind at ease."

"Do you approve?" Hope asked hesitantly.

Evelyn paused and considered her words.

"It is practically unheard of, a situation between a similarly ranked and impoverished lady as yourself, and a Duke. But I can think of no objections to your marriage, apart from that one. Novelty is not immoral, and I can see no reason for the marriage to be objected to."

"Oh, Evelyn, I'm so happy."

Hope buried her face in her cousin's shoulder, almost crying from relief and happiness. Evelyn patted her comfortingly and laughed.

"There, there! No tears; this is a most happy turn of events. We shall have to visit your mother with His Grace so that he can ask for her blessing."

Hope smiled tearfully and nodded. But then, it struck her — they could not possibly let the Duke... Xavier... see her mother's house! Not whilst it was mostly empty of furniture. For to do so would make the stark exigency of Hope's family situation all too clear. She would tell him of the situation in good time, but that was not, at all, the way for him to discover it.

"Perhaps, we should arrange for Mother to visit you, here? That way, the Duke will not need to see the shockingly parlous state to which she has been reduced."

"Very true, and very sensible, Hope. I will set about arranging that. For now, you must rest, and consider everything which will need to be prepared for your wedding. The Duke left this for you."

Evelyn proffered the note, and Hope took it, quickly opening it.

"He will call the day after tomorrow! I already long to see him again."

Evelyn laughed softly.

"So, you are truly taken with him, then? You have not just accepted his offer to save your mother?"

"If I am to be truthful, at first, I thought to do just that… but… the more I saw of him, the more I became intrigued by him, the more I realised that he was quite different from other gentlemen, and the more I came to care for him."

"Good. Let us hope that care becomes love, on both sides of this marriage to be."

Chapter Eight

All that night Hope's thoughts were occupied by beautiful visions of her future life, and she hardly slept a wink, her mind was so filled with ideas.

She could provide for her mother, and perhaps move her closer to Xavier and herself. The house they had received from her father's estate was hardly worth holding on to, for it had been long unused before his death, and would require more work and expenses than it was worth at this point, if Hope could arrange something better for her mother.

A plan began to form in her mind, and she decided, as she finally drifted into sleep, to discuss it with Evelyn in the morning.

The morning, however, made that impossible. Charlotte woke Hope as usual, but there was a worried expression on the maid's face.

"What is it, Charlotte? You look worried."

"Oh, Lady Hope!"

The girl looked truly nervous, and Hope resolved to be as kind to her as possible today.

"Yes? Do tell me what concerns you, Charlotte."

"I'm so worried, every time I think about it. Lady Mainthorpe was called away, very early. It seems that Lady Tennant is having a baby right at this instant, and that the baby has arrived much earlier than expected. Unconventional as it is, Lady Tennant asked for the support of her friend." Charlotte shook her head doubtfully and bit her lip. "Begging your pardon, my Lady, but I didn't know a woman of her age could still bear children – why, she's over forty, and such a small woman! Do you think that she'll be alright?"

Hope nodded, but her thoughts were not truly on the delicate Lady Tennant, much though she commended Charlotte for worrying on the woman's behalf.

She had planned to verify the plan which had come to her in the night, by discussing it with her cousin first, but she was too impatient to wait for Evelyn to return. Having finally thought of a way to help her mother, to ensure her future, she wanted to immediately put that plan into action.

As Charlotte did up the buttons of her gown, she realised that it may even be better if Evelyn didn't know what she was planning on doing. Hope was almost certain that, if Evelyn knew that she wanted to sell her mother's home, she would want to make Hope discuss the idea with her mother before acting on it. But for all her tender and virtuous qualities, Hope's mother did have one fault – she was incredibly stubborn, especially about letting go – of anything. That was a reaction, Hope had come to understand, which had been created in response to the ease with which her father had let things slip away from him. Understandable, but not helpful, now.

Hope knew that the only way their family would be able to pay their debts off and prevent themselves reaching the point where the house was taken from them anyway, leaving them homeless and starving, was if Hope went ahead and sold the property.

If she made sure that there was a clause in the sale documents, which allowed them two months to vacate the property, after the payment had been received, then she would have time, and funds, to arrange for her mother to live somewhere better – close to her, and Xavier.

If they didn't pay off the remaining debts, she knew that their house would be taken from them soon anyway – far better to sell it themselves. And, although Hope was a woman, and had not reached her majority, her mother had, upon falling into illness, arranged with their man-of-business that Hope had full authority to act on her mother's behalf. It was a degree of forethought for which Hope was very grateful, now.

"Yes, I hope so." Hope said, answering Charlotte's question, even as she came to a decision about her day. "I'm going to see Mr. Jenkins, our man of business, today."

"But, my Lady, should you not wait for Lady Mainthorpe to return, to go with you?"

Hope waved away the maid's concerns, hoping that she appeared confident.

"Don't worry, Charlotte, I'll be fine. It's not far. I will take a footman with me, and catch a hackney cab."

"On your own, though, my Lady – with just a footman?"

Charlotte finished buttoning Hope's gown, and urged her to sit in front of the mirror, so that she might dress her hair.

"I'm sure that my cousin will understand."

Hope was not truly that sure of the matter, but she wanted to convince the maid – and, to some extent, herself. She had never actually done something like this before, but being newly betrothed made her feel as if she could do anything.

She had a hasty breakfast, then, footman following, walked down the early morning street and hailed a cab to take them to Mr. Jenkins, the man of business', office.

Mr Jenkins was short, balding, and round. He seemed surprised when Hope arrived, for although he had met her before, and was aware of her authority, he was clearly unused to young ladies seeing him about selling their families' estates. Nonetheless, he agreed to look into the matter for her. With a deep bow, Mr. Jenkins then escorted her out, and Hope felt quite proud of herself as she asked him, before departing, whether he might send to her as soon as he received news.

Hope was back at the townhouse in time to take off her hat and gloves and settle in with tea before Evelyn returned, with tales to tell of Lady Tennant's bravery, and the successful delivery of a baby boy.

The next week passed uneventfully, apart from the fact that Hope felt as though she was living in a dream. Evelyn gave the Duke permission to call once a day, which he did, to take tea with them. Hope and her cousin learned much more about him - his upbringing, childhood, and the subject closest to his heart – his tenants and estates. Hope's respect for Xavier grew as she saw the passion with which he described his day to day responsibilities in caring for his tenants. Hope had not thought that such a wealthy man could actually be concerned about the small lives of ordinary farmers and such, but it was obvious that he cared a great deal.

She could see that her cousin was begrudgingly gaining an admiration for the Duke too. It seemed as though everything was going perfectly. Evelyn had sent her mother a letter informing her about the sudden but fortunate betrothal, and Lady Salenton had replied, with more vigour and enthusiasm than Hope had seen from her since her father's death, demanding to meet the young man.

Plans had now been made for Lady Salenton to visit Evelyn and meet Xavier late in the following week, leaving Mrs. Stoughton to care for Cherrywood Manor in her absence.

Hope's secret plans also seemed to be progressing without any difficulties when Mr. Jenkins called on her, early in the week of her mother's visit. Evelyn was supervising the changing of the drapes in the parlour, in honour of Lady Salenton and the Duke's meeting, when Mr. Jenkins knocked on the door and was admitted by the footman. Hope was passing through the hall and quickly intercepted the solicitor.

"It's all right, Potter. There's no need to bother my cousin." She whispered to the solicitor, "Can you please meet me in the park in the square?"

He looked surprised, but agreed. Hope made sure that her cousin was preoccupied, then hurried out into the park to speak with the man of business.

"What news?" she asked eagerly.

"Less, much less than I expected we might get for the place. You may make the ultimate decision, of course. But you did get an offer, and it is, given the work that would need to be done on the building, quite fair."

He named the figure, but it meant little to Hope.

"Is it enough to pay off our debts – everything that remains, after what the creditors already took from us?"

She waited, hoping and fearing his answer.

"Just, with enough left for the two months of expenses, before your mother must vacate the premises."

Hope let out a breath of relief.

She had feared being an embarrassment or a weight on Xavier, and she had been worrying about having to ask her soon-to-be husband, immediately after their marriage, to pay off the last of her father's debts. It seemed as though everything would work out, and Xavier wouldn't even have to know about the outstanding debts. She did not want him to think that her love was false, that all she cared about was money – for that was far from the truth.

If she could not arrange for her mother to live with, or near, herself and Xavier, then Lady Salenton would just have to stay with Evelyn for a while, as Evelyn had offered, many times.

"Pray go ahead and sell the estate and pay off my father's debts. I will dismiss the servants at the appropriate time, and my mother will move out before the two months is up."

"Shouldn't I speak to Lady Salenton?" Mr. Jenkins asked, a bit dubiously.

"No!" Hope exclaimed. "Erm... all will be well – I will notify her of our progress on the matter."

He nodded doubtfully, but assured her that the sale of the estate could be finalised and the debts paid off immediately. Hope nodded in relief and thanked him.

Chapter Nine

Xavier moved through the days as if in a dream. His mother was pleased, he was happy, and Lady Hope seemed happy as well. Every day, he cared for her more, and she seemed to feel the same. The time spent with her became the highlight of each day. The banns were called in the church near Chatterley Park, for he wanted to marry there, away from London, and near all that was closest to his heart.

And, thankfully, he need no longer endure balls and soirees – having found a woman he wanted to marry, there was no reason to do so. Smith called on him, a week or so after the betrothal had been arranged, bringing further information. He brought the man into his study, and closed the door, waving Smith to a chair.

"Your Grace, I have uncovered more detail about Lady Hope Spencer's father. The Earl of Salenton was, indeed, a gambler, and latterly, a drunkard. The scandal around his death, which I had not uncovered the detail of before, related to just how and where he died."

"I see – and just where was it?"

"He was found in an alley, outside a well-known gaming hell. Stabbed, and his throat cut. His clothes reeked of gin, according to the report of the men who found him. No one ever discovered who killed him, and apparently there were a number of possibilities, for he owed substantial debts to quite a few undesirable moneylenders. I understand that the current Earl, who is a third cousin, went to the extent of having it all hushed up, so as not to taint his own reputation, but was not so generous as to pay out the debts. Those fell to Lady Salenton and her daughter, as part of their 'inheritance' – which was minimal anyway, being a single house and its land, and the last dregs of her dowry, which were held in trust."

Xavier regarded Smith for a moment with some shock.

"I would say, if that is the case, that the current Earl of Salenton is somewhat of a cad, to leave his relatives with debt like that to deal with."

"Indeed, Your Grace."

"And... has the debt been dealt with? Or does it hang over Lady Hope and her mother still?"

"Sadly, Your Grace, I do not believe that it has all been dealt with. Some has been, and I believe that certain creditors have not been backward in confiscating much of the removable items from Lady Salenton's home, but there seem to be other debts as yet unresolved. I am attempting to discover the truth of it, in detail, now."

"Let me know, as soon as you have that detail, so that we can create a plan to deal with it, with finality. I will not allow my betrothed's mother to be beggared because her husband's third cousin is a cad."

"Yes, Your Grace."

They spoke for a little longer, then Smith went on his way, and Xavier sat, considering what he had learned.

It made him, he realised, even more appreciative of Lady Hope. For, of a certainty, if creditors had stripped items of value from her mother's house, then she knew at least to some degree, the straights her mother had been left in. Yet she had not mentioned it, had made no attempt to ask him for money, or to seek anything from him beyond his company.

That she might care for him, for himself, left him feeling warmed and happy, every time that he considered it. He would do all that he could to help her mother, now, simply because she had not asked, had neither demanded, nor expected it of him, immediately they had become betrothed.

*****

The day of Lady Salenton's visit came quickly. Hope was excited to see her mother again and share the happiness of her betrothal. Xavier had already arrived, and had been given permission by Evelyn to take Hope for a walk in the park, to give her mother time to arrive, settle in and ready herself for the afternoon tea meeting.

Evelyn had sent her own carriage for Lady Salenton, who had taken the journey slowly, staying in an Inn overnight, and then coming the last part of the distance this very morning, so that she would not be exhausted when she arrived.

Hope greatly enjoyed the walk with her betrothed, who whispered all sorts of delightful and nonsensical things to her.

It felt as though, over the past few weeks, she had come to know the Duke as well as she knew herself. Xavier assured her, as often as she allowed him to, that he had 'never known anyone as beautiful, honest, or authentic'.

They returned to the townhouse smiling at each other like fools, oblivious to the world.

"Hope!" her mother called to her from inside the parlour. Hope broke away from Xavier and rushed into the sunny room to see her mother comfortably situated in an armchair, her lap covered by a blanket. Minutes later, as the two broke apart after a long hug, Hope took a good look at her mother, who she hadn't seen for three long months. Alice, Lady Salenton, still looked ill, but less so, and now she had a hopeful spark in her eyes and a happy smile. "My Hope, I am so happy for you."

Her voice wavered as she spoke, and Hope suspected that she was close to tears. Hope turned and gestured to Xavier, who lingered uncertainly in the doorway.

"This is the Duke of Birkchester, Mama," she said.

It was her turn to smile encouragingly to assuage the Duke's fears, for he had told her that he was quite nervous about meeting her mother, wishing to be sure that the lady would find him worthy of her daughter.

"It is truly a pleasure to finally meet you, my Lady. I pray you, do not trouble yourself to rise – let us be as family, now," Xavier said, striding forward and kissing Lady Salenton's hand in a deep bow.

Hope's mother gave him a significantly impressed look as Evelyn entered with Charlotte following behind with the tea service, and the Duke, Evelyn and Hope sat down to talk with Lady Salenton.

Hope had never felt so happy, as she took in the faces of the people whom she most loved, all sitting around her. It looked as though Xavier was making a wonderful first impression on her mother, and an excellent renewed impression on her cousin, as he displayed his impeccable manners and good upbringing. He was a pleasant and pleasing conversationalist, now that he had come to know Evelyn better, as well as a great listener, and Hope felt incredibly proud to call him her betrothed as she observed the laughing faces of her cousin and mother.

"I can never thank you enough for paying off my husband's debts, Your Grace," Lady Salenton was telling the Duke.

His smile faded into an expression of confusion as Evelyn nodded and added her own comment.

"Yes, my aunt told me how surprised she was to receive the news just yesterday, that the last of them had been paid. You really shouldn't have – you are too generous."

Hope was slow to react, for she hadn't anticipated this situation at all – obviously, Mr Jenkins had taken it upon himself to send all of the receipts to her mother. Xavier looked flabbergasted and turned to Hope, obviously seeking an explanation.

Hope quickly weighed her options – it would be difficult, at this moment, to break the news that she had sold the family estate. Unwisely, she decided to play the situation by ear and hope that the Duke understood.

"May I speak to you about this later, Your Grace?" she asked Xavier, looking uncomfortable.

To her distress, he abruptly stood up and said, in a strained voice, "I have just recalled something of the utmost importance which I must take care of. Will you please excuse me?"

Evelyn and Lady Salenton looked surprised but murmured "Of course."

He quickly bowed to the two women, but barely inclined his head in Hope's direction before seizing his hat from the surprised footman and hurrying out of the door.

"Now, that was odd!" Evelyn exclaimed. "I wonder what that was about."

Hope murmured something unintelligible and ran after the Duke.

"Hope!"

Her mother called to her, but she continued to run - out of the front door, and along the side of the square until she caught up with Xavier, who had already gone a long way.

"X-Xavier!" He turned, and she saw in his face the thought which she had most feared that he would think. She was sure that he was thinking that everything she had done was an act, to fool him into believing that she wasn't after his money, when in actuality the first thing that her family had expected was that he'd pay off their debts. "You – you don't understand."

He looked distressed and when he spoke, his voice was firm.

"No, I do understand. Don't you know that I've been privy to tactics and strategies about marrying for money for my whole life? That's what I hoped to get away from, just once."

"But–"

"It's all right," he said emphatically, taking Hope's hands into his. "It's a fact of life. I just thought that you were different."

With that he let go of her hands and turned on his heel, rapidly disappearing from sight.

Hope stood there, watching him go down the street towards his town house, feeling a tear slip down her cheek.

*****

It was only as he dropped into the chair at his desk, and lifted the brandy glass to his lips, that Xavier thought beyond his disappointment.

He stopped, barely having sipped, and set the glass down.

Yes, he had hoped that Lady Hope was different. Yes, he was disappointed, for obviously, her relatives had been desperately clinging to the possibility of her marrying well, to save them from dire financial straights. But still… something did not make sense.

She had not, ever, asked him for funds, nor expressed a wish that he might rescue her family. And… most importantly, her mother and her cousin had spoken of debts having been paid. Yet he had, most definitely, not paid them – even though he had been planning to. Smith had not yet brought him the full list, nor the plan for paying them in such a manner as to guarantee that they were fully paid, and that no underhanded ruffian attempted to extort more from Lady Salenton.

Which meant that someone had paid them.

He could not imagine who, but it was obvious, now that he considered it, that Lady Hope knew something about it.

What had his betrothed done?

And was it something that might put her at risk?

No matter how disappointed he felt, he still cared for her, still planned to marry her – but only after he discovered the truth of what had happened, of who had paid those debts, and how.

Until he had that knowledge, he would not call on her, no matter how the tears on her cheeks had torn at his heart as he had walked away. He had to know the truth, for both of them, if they were to have a successful life together.

****

Suddenly Hope remembered where she was – out in public – and she brushed off her tears and composedly walked back to the house, praying that no-one had seen – but being almost certain that someone would have looked out of their window and watched with avid interest.

She would undoubtedly be the subject of lively gossip for months to come, thanks to the little scene which had just taken place, but she didn't care. All she knew was that she had lost the good opinion of the man she loved, all through her secretiveness and his quick judgement.

Her footsteps dragged as she entered the parlour, dreading the need to explain the debacle to her mother and cousin.

"Hope!"

Hope had expected a scolding, but instead Evelyn gave her a hug and waved down Lady Salenton, who had tried to stand up. Evelyn silently sat Hope down near her mother, and Lady Salenton handed her a cup of warm tea. The two women watched quietly as Hope swallowed most of the drink in a few hasty gulps and leaned back tiredly.

"Oh, Mother," Hope sobbed, hugging her mother, and burying her head in Lady Salenton's shoulder as Evelyn patted her hand. "I've made such an awful mistake."

"Then you must tell us about it, so that we can see what may be done to rectify it."

Hope nodded, swallowed more tea, then began to speak, slowly at first, then faster, as the words poured out of her. Her mother and cousin listened, alternating between expressions of disapproval and sympathy, but thankfully refrained from commenting until the end.

"Well," Evelyn said, sending a hesitant look to Lady Salenton, "we can straighten out the debts and house sale with Mr. Jenkins tomorrow."

"No," Lady Salenton said firmly, setting a comforting hand on Hope's shoulder. "Hope should have discussed the sale with me first, but if she hadn't done what she did, our debts may have driven us out of our home within weeks anyway, so it's all right, dear."

"B-but, where will we live now? Xavier certainly will not want to marry me now."

"That's not true!" Evelyn exclaimed, shaking Hope lovingly and glancing at her mother. "Of course we can explain this misunderstanding. I'm sure he will be reasonable when he hears the truth. And anyway, you know that I have offered, from the very beginning, to have you live with us at Mainthorpe Hall, or in the Hall Dower House. Now that Mainthorpe's mother is gone, it stands empty. There will always be somewhere for you to live."

Lady Salenton sighed.

"You are right, Evelyn. You were right from the beginning – I was just too stubborn, too afraid to change. Now, with the weight of the debts off my mind, I can turn my attention to healing. I am beyond tired of being an invalid."

Hope hugged her mother tightly.

"We will find a way to resolve this, Mother, and you will get well again."

Chapter Ten

Despite their hopes, it seemed that the Duke was not interested in explanations or reasoning. Hope sent him letter after letter, explaining and pleading with him, but received no answer. Finally, faced with the fact that near a week had passed, and she was no further advanced in resolving the issue, she was forced to take drastic action, and go to the Duke's London townhouse.

She had been dreading this part – she was still humiliated by how she had gone chasing down the street after Xavier, and been rejected, and she didn't know how many people had seen that through their windows or when walking past on the street. She imagined that the whole city was talking about her, and the Duke, no doubt guessing that their betrothal was over, or worse.

Hope felt that if, this last time, he wouldn't see her, she should hide from the world and from Xavier forever. But she just *couldn't* give up until she'd had the chance to explain the truth to him, face to face.

She could stand losing him as her betrothed, if it came to that, no matter how much her heart hurt at the thought, but she couldn't stand having Xavier hold the wrong impression of her, having him believe that she had chosen to manipulate him for her own gain. Why did she have to lose him, just as she realised that she truly loved him?

Evelyn accompanied her to the Duke's home a week after the day of the dreadful misunderstanding. Hope felt terribly queasy as they walked up the front steps.

"Let me handle this," Evelyn whispered as she smiled at the butler who had opened the door. "Good afternoon. We would like to see the Duke."

She handed the butler their calling cards.

The butler looked at them appraisingly and Hope blushed and looked down, certain that he knew who she was, and was, at that moment, pitying her.

"Unfortunately, His Grace left earlier this week. He has gone to Lord Ashton's estate."

"Left?" Hope exclaimed in panic, ignoring her cousin's warning look. "But he couldn't have!"

"I can take a message and send it on to the Duke."

"That's quite all right, thank you, that won't be necessary," Evelyn said tartly, ushering Hope back down the steps. They were silent on their way home, as Hope came to terms with the fact that he had abandoned her, without a further word.

By the time that they settled back in the parlour, and told Lady Salenton the terrible news, Hope felt no better – she did not know what to do next – but she had to do something. She could not, simply could not, lose him this way.

Evelyn and Lady Salenton attempted to comfort her, but she would not be consoled.

"Why don't you write to him at his friend's house?"

Evelyn looked at her, awaiting an answer. She shook her head, uncertain.

"Then wait it out," her mother advised. "He may yet return."

Hope was not happy with either answer, but she had no better suggestion. She took herself to her rooms, and curled up to cry, overwhelmed, and exhausted.

*****

He had gone to Ashton's estate, which was not far outside London, to give himself time to think – and to give Smith time to gather the last of the required information. Smith liked a puzzle, and when Xavier had explained the conundrum of Lady Salenton's paid debts, Smith had almost rubbed his hands together.

Now, with the morning post delivered to Ashton's had come a thick bundle of documents from Smith, all sealed in a locked box. It was one of a set of boxes which Xavier had commissioned some years ago – boxes for which only he and Smith had the keys. They had proven their value, time and time again.

He took the box into the small parlour at the back of the ground floor of Ashton's monstrosity of a country house, which he had been using as a study whilst staying there, and unlocked it, pulling out the bundles of papers, and stacking them on the desk.

On the top of the pile in the box was a single sheet, filled with Smith's neat hand.

'Your Grace, these are all of the details of debts which Lord Salenton left, of the materials taken by creditors, and of which amounts were paid, when, and in what manner. You will find the solution to where the final amounts of money came from in the first folder. I believe that the majority of items which were confiscated by creditors, from Lady Salenton's home, will be able to be retrieved. With respect to the matter of the three companies whose value as ongoing investments you questioned, I now have almost everything needed. I will bring those to you tomorrow, in person, so that you may choose your course of action.

Regards

Smith.'

Xavier smiled, and settled in to go through each folder, and each list, taking careful note of all that would need to be done to restore to Lady Salenton what should have rightfully been hers. This, he thought, was a far better use to put some of his money to, than those companies he had asked Smith to investigate.

He would ensure that everything was truly paid, would recover things like furniture and heirloom china, and would have his estate manager refurbish Chesterford Manor, which was a house on the grounds of Chatterley Park, so that Lady Salenton might have a residence of her own, as well as her possessions returned.

Once things were planned, and he had spoken to Smith tomorrow, he would go back to London, and to Lady Hope, and beg her forgiveness for the length of his absence, and the manner of his departure. For, now that Smith had provided him with the evidence of what she had done to dispose of those debts, he was proud of her – proud of her courage and determination, and most proud of the fact that she had arranged it all herself, rather than coming to him, begging.

It was time to apologise to her for his doubts.

✱✱✱✱✱

After a week of moping and sleepless nights, Hope came to a decision. She wouldn't beg, nor demand that he marry her, even though he had promised to do so. A betrothal was not so easily discarded, not when the banns had already been read at least once – so she would simply ask for the consideration of being heard, of having the opportunity to tell her side of the matter. Then he could do whatever he wished.

But… exactly how she was to ask for that consideration, when he was not in London, was the point of difficulty. She watched for anything that she might turn into an opportunity to present her case to the Duke, and a few days later she got her chance.

Evelyn was taking Hope's mother to see her preferred physician, for she feared that the smoggy London air was not good for Lady Salenton's fragile health, and she intended that Lady Salenton should have only the best of care. They would be gone for most of the day.

Hope had begged off accompanying them, citing her propensity to break down in tears at any moment, and her desire to be where the Duke would expect her to be, should he return. Her cousin and mother sympathetically excused her, and after she had kissed them goodbye and watched their carriage disappear down the road, Hope sprang into action.

She called Charlotte, and asked for help to dress in her best day gown, then retrieved the letter she had written days before from her escritoire, and carried it downstairs. As she set it on the correspondence tray, she asked Charlotte to have the second carriage brought around.

"But, Lady Hope—!"

Hope ignored Charlotte's protest, and put on her gloves and hat.

"Please, Charlotte, it's an emergency. And I've let my cousin and mother know."

Which she had - at least in the letter.

"But… Lady Hope, where are you going? Shouldn't I at least come with you?"

Hope fixed the maid with a stern glare (an expression she had learnt from her cousin).

"No Charlotte. I must do this myself. I cannot bear continuing to live in this uncertainty. I must resolve the problem which my own actions created."

"Yes, my Lady. But… I'll not lie, this worries me a great deal."

"Nonetheless, I will still do it. I must see the Duke. Now summon the carriage."

Charlotte bobbed a curtsey, and went to do as she was bidden, worry still etched on her face. Hope waited, nervously twisting her hands together, and wondering, for the thousandth time, if this was a sensible plan, or the height of madness.

Finally, after what seemed an hour, the small carriage rolled up before the front door, driven by Lady Mainthorpe's junior coachman, and with a young footman riding on the back. Hope strode out to it, eager to be on her way.

"To Lord Ashton's estate."

The coachman looked somewhat startled at her instruction, but did not argue. She had made quiet enquiries, and discovered that Lord Ashton's estate was two hours' drive away – not too far from London, but far enough. She stepped up into the carriage, and leant back against the well-padded seat, staring out of the window. The footman shut the door, and she felt the carriage shift as he climbed back on, and then they began to move.

As the stone townhouses and cobblestone streets of London transformed into shady trees and softly rolling land, Hope's mind tried to sort through the jumble of what she wanted to tell Xavier. It was critical that she express herself clearly, that she admit her failings, and beg his forgiveness for the wrongs she had actually done, whilst clarifying the fact that she had, absolutely, not done some things he likely assumed she had.

The rocking of the carriage made her drift towards sleep, even as she tried to sort through things in her mind, and, sooner than she had expected, the carriage turned through imposing gates, rolled down a long, gravelled drive, and came to a stop before an imposing house.

"Oh."

Hope almost lost her nerve, for she so dreaded creating a spectacle of herself and causing more gossip. But she simply had to tell Xavier that she wasn't who he thought she was. That she loved him and wanted to marry him, and that she had done her best to solve her mother's problems herself, rather than ask him to do so.

She steeled herself, gulped, and, after stepping down onto that perfect expanse of gravel, spoke to the coachman.

"Wait here, please. I'll take no more than half an hour, I expect."

"Careful, my Lady. It looks like a bad storm is coming on," he waved upwards to where, indeed, dark clouds were beginning to hide the blue of the late spring sky. "I can wait half an hour, most like, but no more. After that, if those clouds keep rolling in, I'll need to find shelter for the carriage and horses – either in the stables here, if Lord Ashton permits it, or at that Inn we passed not far back."

"Of course. I will be as fast as I may, and will seek you out at one of those locations, if it becomes necessary for you to move."

Twisting her gloves in her hands nervously, she strode up to the front door, held her breath, and rapped the knocker.

Chapter Eleven

Hope waited with tingling nervousness, but no one came to the door. She knocked again, then once more, her nervousness becoming impatience. Time was running out.

Greatly daring, she tried the door handle, but it was locked. Just when she had given up all hope, and was considering exploring the grounds, she heard the faint echo of footsteps, inside. She rapped the knocker again.

Moments later, the door opened, and a young footman peered at her, looking somewhat confused to see a young lady, alone, on the step.

"May I help you, my Lady?"

"I... ah... I need to see the Duke of Birkchester – I believe that he is currently visiting Lord Ashton?"

The footman regarded her with even greater doubt than before, but apparently decided that he should not question the actions of his betters.

"The Duke is in residence, my Lady. I am not certain of his exact location at this moment. There is, you see, a garden party in progress – on the lawns at the rear of the house. All of the servants are out there, attending to the guests. If you will come in, and wait, I will see if I can locate him. Do you have a calling card?"

Hope pulled a card from her reticule, and handed it to the footman. He read it, then waved her in, leading her down the hallway towards the rear of the building. Finally, he stopped, and showed her into a very small parlour, asking her to wait there.

His footsteps retreated, and she found herself immersed in silence. Worry filled her – she had wanted to speak to Xavier privately, but if the footman announced her presence to him, in the midst of a garden party... the very idea made her shiver. She was afraid of embarrassing Xavier, afraid of becoming a scandal he would never forgive her for, but she also felt that she was so close to finding him, and explaining everything, that she could not give up.

The house was eerily quiet, and she felt her half hour rapidly slipping away with every tick of the clock on the mantel. Just as she was beginning to wonder if the footman would ever find him, or if she had been completely forgotten, she heard a raised voice. It seemed to come from the wall to her right, as if someone in the next room was speaking loudly.

It was a voice she thought she recognised... Hope hurried over and put her ear to the wall, shamelessly eavesdropping. The voice came again, and now she was certain - it was Xavier's voice. She went to pull back from the wall, and rush into the hallway seeking the door to that next room, when the sense of what he was saying came clear to her.

"I don't want any arguments, Smith," the Duke was saying impatiently.

"But Your Grace – do you think this is wise – I know that you want to take definitive action, but to cut them off so suddenly… that may not be good for your reputation with other possible…?"

Hope didn't recognise the second voice. Then Xavier spoke again.

"I've made up my mind. You're my solicitor, Smith, not my spiritual counsellor. I want no further contact with them. Cease the payments immediately – I'll not be taken advantage of. If they persist, if they do not agree to cancel the contracts, I will take legal action to nullify those contracts instead. I have better things to do with my money than pour it into such activities."

For a moment, she could not make sense of it at all – what were they talking about? Then a terrifying clarity descended upon her – there was only one thing that he might mean.

Hope stared blankly at the wall, shock filling her.

He had to be talking about the marriage contracts, which had been drawn up by Mr Jenkins, and signed only two weeks earlier. Xavier was going to break their betrothal; and it sounded as though he blamed her for taking advantage of his betrothal offer to extort money. As if he would take legal action against her family… *He must really loathe me to consider such things.*

Everything she had hoped for by coming here seemed utterly pointless in that moment. Explanations would be useless in such a situation – it was apparent that he had already made up his mind – about everything. Dizziness assailed her, and she half fainted, crumpling against the wall with a thump.

She forced herself back to her feet, a hopeless, hollow feeling in the pit of her stomach. Somehow, she managed to turn, to half-run from the room, a sob choking from her throat. She sped past the shocked footman in the hall, and out of the front door, uncaring what he might think of her, suddenly needing, more than anything, to escape.

Thunder rumbled ominously, and it had become quite dark. The first spits of rain touched her face, and mingled with her tears. Her carriage was barely in sight, just turning out of the gates at the end of the long drive, obviously hurrying back to that Inn, to shelter the horses. No doubt, because of the garden party, the stables here were full.

With the thought that her life could hardly grow any worse, Hope began running down the drive, in the direction which the carriage had taken, fleeing from the destruction of her every dream.

✳✳✳✳✳

"As you wish, Your Grace. I will inform the companies tomorrow of your decision, and of the fact that, should they argue the case, you will pursue them for the return of every penny you've invested to date. I doubt that, given what we've discovered about them..."

Smith never finished the sentence, for a loud thump echoed through the room. A thump which seemed to come from the wall between the room they were in, and the next small parlour along the hall.

Xavier and Smith exchanged startled looks.

Moments later, Xavier heard the click of a door, and running footsteps in the hall. What on earth was going on? Had someone been eavesdropping on his business meeting? But if so, why?

"Wait here, Smith."

Xavier flung himself into the hallway, and barely avoided colliding with a young footman.

"Your Grace!"

"Who was in this room?"

Xavier waved his hand at the relevant door, and glowered at the footman, who paled.

"A Lady, Your Grace. She wanted to see you, and I didn't know where you were, so I asked her to wait in there."

"A Lady? Who?"

The footman proffered a calling card in a shaking hand, and Xavier almost snatched it from him. For a moment, as he looked at it, the words on it made no sense – but then, they came into sharp focus.

Lady Hope Spencer.

She had come here, looking for him. His own fault, for he had left it far too long to return to her, far too long to apologise for his mistaken assumptions. But... where was she now? And what had happened, to cause that thump on the wall? Obviously, he had frozen on the spot, for the footman's voice came again, hesitant, and worried.

"Your Grace?"

"Where is she now?"

The footman waved a hand towards the front door, frowning.

"I ah, saw her run off, Your Grace. She ran out of the room, and off down the hall, then out the door, as if the hounds of Hell were chasing her, if you'll forgive the expression. Near trampled me as she went."

At that moment, a great clap of thunder sounded overhead, and the fanlight above the front door was lit by the flash of lightning. Hope, his Hope, was out there, in that... he could not allow it, could not let her run off, thinking who knew what. What did she think? Had she heard what he had been discussing with Smith, and somehow misinterpreted it? Or was something else wrong?

It did not matter – all that mattered was that he find her, that he tell her how much he loved her, that he had been wrong to judge her.

"Send to the stables – have my horse saddled and brought around immediately."

"Y... Your Grace? But it's raining...?"

"Exactly. And Lady Hope is out there, in that rain. Hurry man!"

The footman ran off, even as Xavier sprinted up the stairs, to change into his boots, and grab his tiered shoulder greatcoat and his hat. If he was to chase his beloved in the rain, at least he would be a little better than completely soaked.

✶✶✶✶✶

There was a bright flash of lightning and an especially loud rumble of thunder, then it suddenly began to rain in heavy, driving sheets.

Hope's tears mixed with the freezing cold rain as she tripped and fell, her best day gown getting covered in muddy smears from the gravel, her knees hurting, and quite likely grazed, even through the fabric of her gown.

There would be a scandal.

Xavier was going to break their betrothal, and cause the final ruin of Hope and her family, she was sure. Public opinion would be against them. Her family name would be ruined, Evelyn's life in London would be ruined, perhaps Lord Mainthorpe's business investments too, if he demanded financial compensation. No one would hear her side of the story, since she was, despite being the daughter of an Earl, at this point an impoverished, fatherless nobody.

How was it that little more than a week ago, she was happily planning her wedding, feeling loved for the first time in her life, and now...?

She lay there in the dirt, oblivious to the wet and cold, gathering her strength to push to her feet and go on. After all, what else could she do? Then, she heard hoofbeats.

Lifting her head and wiping her eyes, Hope peered towards the house, and could barely make out a horse and rider approaching. She scrambled up – was someone coming to find out why she had been there? She could not face explaining, could not face yet more disaster.

She turned back towards the gates, and began running, but slipped on the slick mud and pebbles, falling again. She was attempting to struggle up when the horse reached her. The rider swung down and started towards her, Hope watched through the rain, unable to believe her eyes.

"Xavier!"

He tried to hold her, to lift her up to her feet, but she pushed away his hands and cried out.

"Don't touch me! I've done nothing wrong. I want nothing from you. I tried so hard to deal with it all myself! Why won't you leave my family alone?"

"What are you talking about?" Xavier yelled, straining to be heard through the pouring rain. "I love you!"

"You don't love me," Hope sobbed, scrambling back away from him. "You loathe me. You have to loathe me, if you really think that I would try to extort money from you. If you sue me, you will win, but you will be in the wrong. I don't want a shilling of your money."

"Sue you?" Xavier shouted over the rain, coming towards her again. "You've got it all wrong!"

He seized her hands and she stopped resisting, head bowed and quietly sobbing as the driving rain stung her cheeks, and turned her hair to a tangle of knots.

"I h-heard you telling your solicitor everything."

"Hope." Hope looked up. They could barely see each other in the heavy rain, but Xavier stepped closer and pushed her hair gently away from her face. His voice was tender. "I was telling my solicitor to cancel some old investments of mine – things which no longer serve my estate, because the companies I had been dealing with turned out to be less than honest in their business dealings – which is why we may need to threaten them with legal action, to prevent them being tempted to try anything underhanded. Recovering those funds will allow me to pay whatever you and your family need me to, instead – a far better investment, in my opinion."

"What?"

Hope peered up at him, unable to understand. Xavier came even closer, his arms slowly wrapping around her, folding the sides of his greatcoat about her shivering body. She leant into his warmth, even as she studied his face, her own a picture of confusion.

"Did you think I could treat you so cruelly, my lamb?"

"But you were angry with me," Hope said, unable to keep a note of accusation from her voice. "You were disappointed."

Xavier nodded solemnly.

"I know. Will you ever forgive me?" Hope wiped the tears and rain out of her eyes and peered up at him wonderingly, beginning, just beginning, to dare to believe that everything might be all right, as he continued speaking. "I didn't love you as I ought to have. I was in love with what I thought you should be, the fantasy that I had built in my mind. That's why I ran away here to Ashton's house to clear my head, and to think through what had really happened. I realised that I was wrong, that somehow, you had managed to pay those debts yourself, as a surprise to your mother and cousin – I could make no other conclusion from what they said that day, when I stopped and truly thought. I asked Smith to confirm that for me, and I began to make plans to apologise to you, to do all that I could to improve your mother's life, as well as yours. I love *you*, no matter your motivations in marrying me. I'm proud of the strength you've shown, by achieving what you did. I don't care if at first you may have considered my money – you never asked me for it. Will you ever forgive me?"

In answer, Hope turned her face up to his. Xavier slowly lowered his lips to hers, and kissed her, in a manner which made her completely forget that they stood in the pouring rain. But, after a moment, Hope broke away and smiled.

"There is nothing to forgive, Xavier. And... I hope that you have nothing to forgive me for, either." The Duke looked confused, and she went on, "There has been a misunderstanding about the debts, one that, from what you have just said, you already have some insight into, but I wish to explain it to you. I want there to be no misperceptions between us, from this day on. But... would you please take me back to my cousin's? I promise to explain everything once we get there. I came in her second carriage, but the coachman warned me that he would need to go to the Inn we had passed, to find shelter for the horses and carriage, if the storm overcame us."

"Of course, how inconsiderate of me - there will be time to talk once you are warm and dry. Normally, I would suggest that I mount, and that you perhaps ride behind me, as sitting behind the saddle is likely far more comfortable than across the pommel in front. But... I do not think that asking you to sit on a very damp horse is a polite request to make of a Lady!"

Hope laughed.

"Then what do you propose, Xavier?"

"I will mount, and if you use that log over there as a mounting block, we should be able to get you settled sideways in front of me, sitting across my thighs. I can wrap my coat around you, as well as my arms, and keep you at least a little warm as we go back to the house."

"That seems sensible."

Soon, they had done as he suggested, and Xavier wrapped his arms around her as she laid her head against his chest, utterly content, and they rode slowly back down the drive.

Chapter Twelve

The next hour was rather a blur, as Hope allowed herself to be cared for, and rapid arrangements were made. The storm passed, fading to a light drizzle of ongoing rain, and by the time that Xavier's carriage had been readied, and his possessions loaded into it, she was mostly dry, having spent that time curled in front of a fire, wrapped in blankets.

Xavier had brushed away all enquiries from other guests at Lord Ashton's estate, and simply demanded what he wanted. The only other person she saw, apart from the servants who brought her a warm drink and more blankets, was Lord Ashton himself, who came to make certain that his guest was being well cared for. When Xavier returned to the room, smiling, she was more than ready to leave.

"The carriage is ready, my love. There is a heated brick to keep your feet warm, and more blankets. I have sent a footman to the Inn with a message for Lady Mainthorpe's coachman, so that he should be prepared, and ready to follow us to London, once we reach him."

He gently folded the blankets back from her shoulders, and offered a large cloak – which must have been one of his own. She stood, and accepted it gratefully.

"Thank you, Xavier. I feel much improved for being warm."

"Then let us go – we can talk in the carriage."

Hope took his hand, and allowed herself to be led from the room, through the house, and out to the carriage. Xavier's carriage was, as might be expected, rather more luxurious than her cousin's, or, for that matter, any carriage she had ever travelled in before.

She sighed, leaning back against the soft padded seat, and watched the rain drenched trees along the drive passing by. When they reached the spot where Xavier had found her, in the storm, she turned to him.

"Xavier – what will happen to your horse? Was it one of Lord Ashton's?"

He laughed, shaking his head.

"You are ever the practical one, aren't you? No, the horse is not Lord Ashton's – it is one of mine, my favourite. My groom will ride him back to London, in a few days, once the weather clears. But... might we now talk of the misunderstandings which grew between us? I would learn the truth of everything, that we might not make such mistakes again."

Hope took a deep breath as, for a moment, fear filled her. Then, she gathered her courage and nodded.

"Yes, let us do so. I would have only honesty between us."

Xavier took her hand, and that touch sent warmth through her entire body.

"Tell me about your life, Hope, and how you came to the situation you face."

"I… in truth, I do not entirely know the detail of much of it, for when I was younger, my mother kept it from me, to protect me. It was only when my father died that I began to understand the truth of things. I was fifteen, I had barely seen him for years, but I did not know if that was simply because he was busy with estate business and the like, or something more – many girls rarely see their fathers, after all. But when he died, I discovered that he had been absent because he had been gambling – and that we were far worse off than I had known. All but one property was entailed, and went with the title to Father's third cousin. Mother received one house, and a tiny sum of money – for he had spent the rest -- and I received almost nothing, for the same reason."

Xavier reached out, and brushed a gentle hand over her cheek.

"That is terrible! What did you do?"

"I learnt – a lot, very fast. My mother took ill – partly from grief and the shock of discovering just how poor we were, and partly from the chill that winter, in a house which we could not afford to heat properly. So I became the lady of the house, for all intents and purposes – I learnt how to manage a household, and how to stretch what funds we had. But that year, Evelyn came to see us – her mother and mine have been distant with each other for many years, so to see her was a surprise, but I was very grateful that she wanted to help. She taught me all that I needed to know to be accepted in society. By the time I came to London for this Season, I understood that, despite hoping for love, I needed to marry well, for what funds we had were nigh on exhausted, and the creditors had become more than pressing."

"I see. And yet, that first time that I asked you to marry me, you refused. Why? Surely, if your circumstances were so dire…?"

"Why? Because I was, by any sensible measure, being a fool. I had discovered that I wanted love, or at least liking, and I felt confused by the fact that you would ask, when we had barely met. But then, after that day in the park, I received a letter from my mother. A letter which informed me that creditors had descended on the house, their patience exhausted, and carried off almost everything of value – right down to the furnishings. The shock of that letter was intense – and although Evelyn made sure that my mother had at least funds to carry on with, in the short term, I knew then that I should have accepted you, that I could not afford to be fussy, when my mother's health and home was at stake. So I determined to speak with you, and to convince you, somehow, to make your offer again."

"Whilst I am saddened to think that I held so little appeal for you… I do understand, when you explain it that way."

"I should hope so – for, if I remember that first offer you made me, you expressed it in terms of our being perhaps kindred souls who could go along together well, rather than in terms of any stronger emotions…"

Xavier laughed ruefully.

"Indeed, I did – but every time I saw you, you intrigued me more, I cared for you more, and that faint interest became strong liking, and then love."

"Which is, very much, what happened for me, too. Each time I saw you, I liked you more – and I became more and more conflicted, especially when you spoke of my being different, and not just wanting to marry you for your money and title."

"So… you decided that you had to solve the problem in some manner which did not involve my money?"

"Yes. The more I thought of it, the more it seemed that the only option was to sell the house, before it was taken from us anyway. Evelyn had long ago offered mother the Dower House on Lord Mainthorpe's estate, so I knew that there would be somewhere for mother to live. Mother had given me the authority to act for her, with our man of business, not long after she fell ill – so I knew that I could do this. And I wanted it to be a secret, for Mother can be stubborn, and I knew that we did not have much time, before the last of the debts fell due. Once the house was sold, Mother's practicality would take hold, and she would accept the inevitable. And that way, I would not be asking you for money."

Xavier lifted her hand to his lips and pressed a kiss to it.

"And all went well, until your mother and cousin inadvertently revealed it all to me, too early, and in the worst possible way – and I, fool that I was, instantly made all of the wrong assumptions."

"Yes – for I had not yet told either of them. Mr Jenkins, our man of business, in his eagerness, had sent the final receipts and documents to my mother, instead of to me – and I was not aware that he had done so, until she spoke of it in front of you. I panicked, for I feared that you would make the exact assumption that you did – and by then, I knew that I loved you, knew that I could not bear to lose you."

Xavier laughed.

"We are so similar, my dear Hope. I admit that I rushed off, full of annoyance. But, as soon as I stopped to think, even a little, I realised that it did not make sense."

"Oh?"

"Your mother and cousin had spoken of debts already paid – yet I had made no payments. Which meant that you must have done something, something completely unexpected. So… I asked Smith to discover the details of both the debts, and of how they had been expunged. He is an excellent man of business – he tracked it all down. And as soon as I began to understand the scale of it – which was only in the last few days, at Ashton's, when he brought the papers to me – I set things in motion to not only ensure your mother's future health and home, but to recover as much as I could of the items that the creditors had taken. I wanted it to be my wedding gift to you."

"But… I thought that you would cry off, after the way that you left me there, and did not answer my letters…"

"Letters? I saw no letters. They are likely still at Harte House, waiting for my return. Just today, I had all of the last things arranged, and after my meeting with Smith, I had intended to come back to town, to throw myself at your feet, and beg your forgiveness for my unjust assumptions."

"Oh! And I came to see you, to attempt to at least get you to let me explain – for whilst I would have accepted you crying off, even though it broke my heart, I could not bear the idea that you would believe me simply a money seeker, when I love you."

"Shall we, then, forgive each other, and move on from this, to live a happy married life with no secrets between us?"

"Yes, oh yes."

Hope felt that her heart would burst with happiness, and relief – for to have explained, and had her words accepted, had lifted a great weight from her thoughts. And to know that he had already planned to help her mother!

He pulled her into his arms, and brought his lips to hers, the kiss slow and thorough, gentle at first, and then deepening with passion. It was more than she had ever imagined a kiss could be, and held so much promise for the future.

✱✱✱✱✱

When the carriage drew up in front of Lady Mainthorpe's townhouse, Xavier found himself remarkably nervous. Although all was well between Hope and himself, he would no doubt face a lot of questions from Lady Mainthorpe and Lady Salenton – and rightly so.

The footman opened the door, and let down the steps, and he realised, as he helped Hope out of the carriage, just how totally bedraggled she looked. He'd had the advantage of a change of clothes on hand, but she had not. He hoped that the ladies would not castigate her for her appearance. Nonetheless, he could not help the wide smile which settled on his face – a smile matched by Hope's, as she took his hand, and led him up the steps, to smartly rap the knocker.

Lady Mainthorpe's butler opened the door, and took in Hope's state with a raised eyebrow, but did nothing more than step back and allow them entry. As the door closed behind them, Lady Mainthorpe appeared from the parlour, her expression concerned. Beside him, he felt Hope draw herself up.

"Dear cousin, all will be explained – and let me assure you that those explanations are full of happiness. But first, I must, really must, bathe and change. I entreat you to simply provide His Grace with tea and company, and ask him not one question until I come back down."

With that, she sped off up the stairs, leaving Xavier standing, rather awkwardly, with Lady Mainthorpe, who regained her composure far faster than he did.

"Well! Do come into the parlour, Your Grace. I do declare that I shall likely die of curiosity, before that girl comes back down!"

Xavier laughed, all awkwardness gone in the instant.

"Then I shall simply have to entertain you as I sip my tea – I do hope that there is tea? – with tales of my various estates – isn't that what many gentlemen of the *ton* talk about, incessantly?"

Lady Mainthorpe granted him a conspiratorial grin, and nodded.

"Of course it is, Your Grace – but I suspect that your tales will be a good deal more interesting than most. And yes, there is tea, but," and she turned to the butler, who stood there still, impassive, "Dobson, please have Charlotte bring up a fresh tea tray, with some cakes as well."

*****

Almost an hour later, Hope entered the parlour, feeling refreshed and far more respectable. She wondered just how well Xavier had fared – it had been rather naughty of her to abandon him to her cousin so. The scene which greeted her was peaceful, and more than she had hoped for. They were obviously on their second or third tea tray, and seemed to be discussing the seasonal schedule for repairing tenants' cottages.

She went to sit on the couch beside Xavier, and he took her hand, entwining their fingers. Evelyn looked at her, set her teacup down, and spoke, putting on a long-suffering expression.

"Now that you are here, do, please, explain where you were. I was so worried when we came home to find your note! I gather, from His Grace's presence here, and your happy faces, that all conflict has been resolved?"

"It has indeed. Let me tell you the story from the start…"

Two hours later, Hope and Xavier stopped talking, and Lady Salenton wiped a happy tear from her eye, in response to their declarations of love for each other, and to the news that there was a home for her, set aside on the Duke's estate.

"Well – you are even more generous a man than I had thought to begin with, Your Grace. We had best call upon your mother, and see to making sure that this wedding will be the best it can possibly be."

✳✳✳✳✳

Two days later, as Hope waited for the modiste to call to discuss the finer details of her wedding dress, she heard a carriage draw up and, thinking that it might be Xavier, went to look out of the window. But it was not Xavier – it was Lord Mainthorpe, finally returned from his travels for his estates. Hope hurried down the hall, and burst into the parlour.

"Evelyn, Lord Mainthorpe has returned!"

Her cousin leapt up, her face flushed, and Hope saw, in that moment, what she had always suspected – Evelyn did, truly, love her husband.

Moments later, Lord Mainthorpe came into the room, and greeted his wife with a kiss on the cheek – but his expression said that he intended to do far more than that, as soon as they were private.

Evelyn looked up at him, smiling.

"My dear Mainthorpe, I am so glad that you have returned. We have a request of you."

"Oh? And what might that be, my dear?"

"Hope is betrothed – to the Duke of Birkchester! – and as she lacks a father, we were hoping that you would agree to walk her down the aisle?"

Mainthorpe turned to Hope with an enormous smile, and bowed.

"I would be delighted, my dear girl."

Chapter Thirteen

The church in the village of Chatterley Grove was full – not just with those friends and family of Hope and the Duke, but also with the inhabitants of the village and the surrounding district. There were even a few of the *ton*, come from London to see this most talked about match – talked about because it seemed that some of Lord Ashton's guests had seen just enough to generate gossip.

Hope found that she did not care – all that mattered was Xavier, and the fact that she would be, within the hour, his wife. She walked towards him, Lord Mainthorpe at her side, and wondered, for just a moment, if she was dreaming – if all of the last few months had been lived only in her fevered imagination. But no – he was real, this handsome man who loved her, and whom she loved.

She stood beside him, and the vicar began to speak, intoning the words which would bind them together, forever. Her heart filled with utter joy, and she forgot about everything but saying the words she must, at the right time.

Soon, it was done, and they stepped back out into the late spring sunshine, to be greeted with thrown flower petals. Xavier led her to the carriage and she stepped in for the ride back to Chatterley Park for the Wedding Breakfast. He sat beside her, and then was kissing her, almost before the door was closed. Gladly, she returned that kiss, her whole body responding to his touch. The kiss only ended when the carriage drew up outside Chatterley Park.

Xavier led her into the house, and they went up to his private parlour to spend a little time alone before joining all of their guests down in the ballroom. On the table, awaiting their arrival, was a bottle of champagne, and two glasses.

"Shall I pour you some wine, my love?"

"Yes, please."

Hope watched as he opened the bottle, and the fizzy wine bubbled into the glass. He turned and handed it to her, then poured a glass for himself. She sipped, delighted by the sensation of the bubbles on her tongue, and remembered, in that instant, the first time they had met. He lifted his glass, smiling.

"A toast to us – may our life together be far smoother than our courtship."

Hope laughed, the glass wobbling a little in her hand as she did so, and he reached out to steady it.

"It's all right, Xavier – I promise not to spill my wine all over you, this time!"

Epilogue

The manor which Xavier had given to Lady Salenton was lovely. It was comfortable, large enough for her to have all of the room she needed, without being echoingly empty, and staffed with maids, footmen, and a butler, as well as a cook who saw it as her personal duty to ensure that Lady Salenton's health recovered. Xavier also employed a personal physician for her, who made daily visits initially, and then weekly visits as she improved. As a result, her health rapidly became better, and Hope began to believe that her mother might, finally, get back to the way she remembered her being, some years before Lord Salenton's death.

Xavier and Hope spent the vast majority of their time at Chatterley Park, eschewing London, except when they went to visit Evelyn, when she was in town. At first, Hope visited her mother every day, and greatly depended on her for her advice and wisdom, as she learned all that she needed as mistress of estates as vast as Xavier's. But, as her mother healed, and Hope became used to marriage, things changed.

Lady Salenton actually began to call on others in the district, and built herself a circle of true friends – which Hope was very pleased to see. Evelyn and Lord Mainthorpe visited them, even more often than they visited Evelyn. Hope was astounded at how happy she was, at how good life was, without the constant worry of debt hanging over them.

It became obvious, also, that Xavier had been right from the beginning, when he had said that he sensed a kinship of souls between them, for they were very much in tune, and there seemed nothing which might ever cause them to disagree.

Now, two years after the wedding, and the dramatic events which had preceded it, Hope sat in their private parlour, Xavier beside her with his arm around her. In her arms she held their second child, Isabella, who was barely two months old, and on the large rug in front of them, their son, James, played with some carved blocks. She could not imagine being anywhere else, could not imagine being happier.

But that happiness was the result of their conscious intent – as they had said, that day in the carriage after the rain, there was only honesty between them. Misunderstanding would never again be allowed to push them apart.

The End

I hope that you enjoyed
'Her Generous Duke'

You'll find a preview of another of my
books, 'Her Absent Duke' just after the
'About the Author' section of this book.

About the Author

Arietta Richmond has been a compulsive reader and writer all her life. Whilst her reading has covered an enormous range of topics, history has always fascinated her, and historical novels have been amongst her favourite reading.

She has written a wide range of work, from business articles and other non-fiction works (published under a pen name) but fiction has always been a major part of her life. Now, her Regency Historical Romance books are finally being released. The Derbyshire Set is comprised of 11 novels (9 released so far). The 'His Majesty's Hounds' series is comprised of 17 novels, with the last now released.

She also has a number of standalone novels released, and four other series of novels in development. She lives in Australia, and when not reading or writing, likes to travel, and to see in person the places where history happened.

Be the first to know about it when Arietta's next book is released! Sign up to Arietta's newsletter at

http://www.ariettarichmond.com

When you do, you will receive two free subscriber exclusive books - **'A Gift of Love',** which is a prequel to the Derbyshire Set series, and ends on the day that 'The Earl's Unexpected Bride' begins, and **'Madame's Christmas Marquis'** which is an additional story in the His Majesty's Hounds series.

These stories are not for sale anywhere – they are absolutely exclusive to newsletter subscribers!

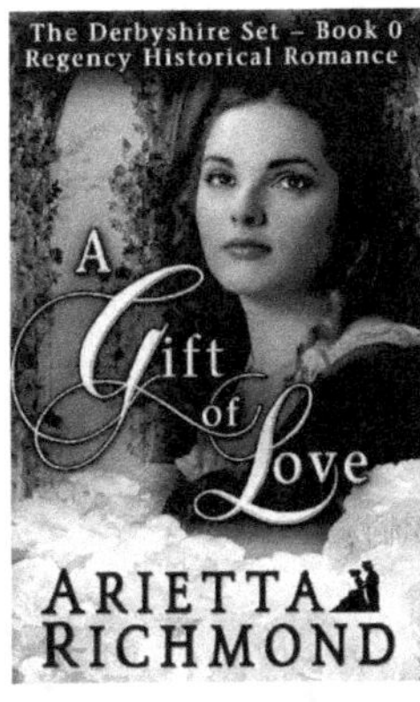

Connect with Arietta:

Donate and support her on Kofi.com
https://ko-fi.com/ariettarichmondauthor

Follow her on Amazon - https://www.amazon.com/Arietta-Richmond/e/B016GG1KJ6/

Like her Facebook Page -
https://www.facebook.com/AriettaRichmondAuthor

Follow her on Twitter - https://twitter.com/AriettaRichmond

Follow her on Instagram -
https://www.instagram.com/AriettaRichmond/

Follow her on Bookbub – https://www.bookbub.com/authors/arietta-richmond

Follow her on Goodreads -
https://www.goodreads.com/author/show/14508806.Arietta_Richmond

Here is your preview of

Her Absent Duke

Clean Regency Romance

Arietta Richmond

 Prologue

1822

Lord Marcus Northam stood at the rail of the ship, watching England recede behind him. His throat felt tight, and bitter sadness filled him.

Had he made the right choice?

He did not know. Only time would tell.

It had been an impossible choice to make, yet he had been forced to make it. He prayed that what he had done was right – but he suspected that, whatever he had chosen, the price which it exacted from him would have been high.

Duty had pulled him in two opposing directions.

Well, he had made a choice, and here he was, doing as he had agreed to do. When, and if, he might ever see England again, he could not know.

Best to turn his eyes forward, instead of back, and accept that, now, his life lay ahead of him, in France or beyond, for the war had left France in disarray, even now, some years later.

Despite his intention to look forward, his mind drifted back, reviewing the life that had brought him to this point. Could he have done anything differently? Could he have avoided this moment?

Perhaps. But he had not – he had allowed himself to be distracted by studying, to bury his doubts in that, rather than paying attention to what was happening in the lives of those he truly cared for. And now it was too late – he could not go back and change any of those things.

She was lost to him.

Until his father's death – and, God willing, that would be many years from now – he could not go back – at that point, it would be different, for his responsibility to the title would take precedence then. But if that was many years away, then it was almost certain that anything he had hoped for would be irreparably changed.

If only life could be simpler, if only he could go back to that idyllic childhood, to the weeks and months he had spent with her, with no thought of anything but a happy future together. If only he could...

But he couldn't.

The wind blew his hair into disarray, and the salt scent of the sea surrounded him, as he relived all of those bittersweet memories. He recalled everything, from the first moment that he had seen her...

Lady Kathryn Harrington woke slowly, and for a moment, all seemed well – until her memory of the previous day came rushing back.

She turned her face into the pillow and the tears came again.

In one day, she had lost everything that she had hoped for, and lost her faith in love and destiny.

He was gone – how could he have done this? She did not understand – nothing in her life had prepared her for such a betrayal, and for its terrible but unintended consequences. All she knew was that it hurt beyond bearing, and that she would never... never!... allow herself to risk such pain again.

But she wished, so very much wished, that it might have been different.

Had she done something, to cause him to act so? Was it all her fault? She did not know, but if there had been a way to go back and make it different, she would have, in a heartbeat.

She should accept her fate, should look forward, not back, yet, despite that intent, her mind kept wandering, remembering, trying desperately to reconcile the boy of her memories with the man who had done this terrible thing.

She could not.

All she could do was to remember, helplessly, hopelessly, the days when a bright future had seemed possible.

She remembered those days well, from the very first time that he had played with her, when she was barely two years old, through every enchanted summer, and every challenging, delightful moment, until the point where he had gone away to school.

She should cast those memories away.

Should accept that they were all false, borne of the unrealistic perceptions of a child.

Should accept that he had never been the man she had thought – for that man could never have done something so terrible.

But somehow, she could not so easily cast him aside. The memories replayed in her thoughts, an endless litany of reminders of joy lost.

Chapter One

1806

Little Lord Marcus Northam looked down at the tiny pink baby swaddled in white muslin, sleeping peacefully in the big ornate cot. He gazed at the sleeping form, watching as its chest rose and fell, and wondered if that's what he'd looked like when he was a baby. His hand bunched as he reached into the cot, and stroked the soft, warm skin. This creature fascinated him and he wanted to feel it.

"Lord Marcus!" the nursemaid hissed, her voice low, as she bustled around him. "Whatever are you doing in here? You are not supposed to be in this room. You'll waken the baby!"

Marcus jumped back, startled, protesting.

"I only wanted to see what it looked like, Bessie!"

Bessie knelt down to look him in the eye, taking hold of his shoulder.

"She's a girl, not an it, Lord Marcus. She's beautiful, isn't she?"

Marcus shrugged and turned his head to look at the still sleeping form.

"It's just a baby, Bessie. Nothing much beautiful about that. And she's just a girl."

Bessie tutted and ruffled his hair.

"Go on Lord Marcus. Go back down the stairs and see your father. You know you're not supposed to be up here on your own."

Marcus sighed and, turning on his heel, ran down the stairs, stopping at the bottom step as he heard his father and His Grace of Scarpdale talking in the parlour. He tiptoed to the slightly ajar door and listened.

Inside the beautifully appointed room, the Duke of Scarpdale, George Harrington, was celebrating the birth of his daughter. Sitting around the room, on elegant silk backed chairs, were his beloved wife, Charlotte, Duchess of Scarpdale, his younger brother, Harold Harrington, the Marquess of Hawthorne, and their closest friends, Julian Northam, the Duke of Weatherly and his wife, Elisabeth, Duchess of Weatherly, who were Lord Marcus' mother and father. Weatherly lifted his glass.

"Well dear friends, we ought to raise our glasses in joyful celebration." He smiled at his close friend, Scarpdale. "What a wonderful occasion this is - the birth of a beautiful baby girl."

Scarpdale smiled graciously and raised his glass.

"To my beautiful wife, Charlotte, for bringing me the most wonderful treasure of all, and to my baby girl. May she have everything she ever wishes for."

They all raised their glasses, then sipped delicately at the fine French champagne. Setting down her glass, Charlotte turned to Elisabeth, smiling.

"Shall we retire to the nursery Elisabeth?"

The Duchess of Weatherly clasped her hands together and beamed

"Why yes! That would be wonderful. I so wish to see your daughter!"

The ladies made their excuses and stood to leave the room. Gasping, Marcus ran and hid behind a pillar, so as not to be discovered listening at the door. The ladies passed him, and he listened to them as they went. The Duchess of Scarpdale was smiling as she spoke.

"I am so glad that we chose to live here, at Harrington Hall, rather than at Scarpdale Chase. This house is so much warmer, so much more welcoming in all ways. It will be a lovely place for a child to grow up. And George has already said that he will have the paperwork done to ensure that this property goes to Kate when we are gone. It's not entailed, so that is not difficult to arrange."

"She's a lucky child then – most girl children do not have such thought given to their future."

They moved up the stairs, and Marcus waited until they had disappeared at the top of the staircase before returning to spy on his father.

He was an inquisitive boy - at only four years old, he was naturally very interested in everything which was going on around him. He loved to watch what was happening, even if he didn't understand much of what was being said at times.

He was standing behind the door, peeking through, when he heard a familiar sniff, then a violent sneeze. He turned to see Henry Harrington, who was the son of the Marquess of Hawthorne, wiping his nose on a voluminous white handkerchief.

"Whatever are you doing out here, Marcus?" Henry's voice had a nasal tone to it, and an edge of nastiness as well. Marcus studied the boy. Although Henry was two years older than him, he didn't look older. He was a scrawny little boy, prone to illnesses, and always had a deathly pale pallor to his face, in stark comparison to Marcus' glowingly healthy countenance. "Are you spying?" Henry spat the words out.

For some reason, Henry didn't seem to like Marcus very much, which was fine by Marcus, because he was not altogether sure that he liked Henry either. Marcus put his hands on his hips and tilted his chin up.

"What does it have to do with you if I am spying, Henry?"

Henry raised his eyebrows in surprise then threw back his head with a triumphant laugh. He grabbed Marcus and dragged him through the door of the parlour.

The men inside stopped their conversation and turned as Henry marched little Marcus to the centre of the room.

"Look who I found lurking outside, Papa!" he exclaimed. "He was spying on you, the naughty little boy."

Henry stood proudly, obviously expecting to be praised for his actions, holding Marcus up by the back of his collar, the effect slightly diminished by the fact that Henry sniffled every few seconds. The men laughed a little as Marcus struggled against Henry, finally breaking free and running to his father. The Duke of Weatherly scooped Marcus into his arms.

"Are you being a naughty boy?"

A playful smile crossed the Duke's lips. Marcus shook his head vigorously.

"No, Papa. I was just interested to hear what was happening. I was sleuthing!"

Hawthorne snorted and sneered.

"Doesn't the child understand that sleuthing is the same as spying?"

Scarpdale looked at his brother and shook his head.

"Leave him be. He's just a babe. It's good that he's inquisitive. I'm more concerned that Henry thought it appropriate to inform on him."

Hawthorne rolled his eyes and motioned for his son to come to him. Henry skulked towards his father and looked at him sullenly. The tension in the room was growing, and Marcus wondered what would happen, when his father turned to Scarpdale and cleared his throat.

"Ah... Scarpdale..."

Marcus looked at his father's face, as the man surveyed his closest friend, and wondered why his father seemed uncertain. Usually, his father was quite sure about everything – at least from Marcus' perspective. Scarpdale looked at Weatherly, a benevolent smile playing across his face.

"Yes, what is it, my friend?"

"Ahem, well. You know that we have been friends for longer than I care to remember. You have been there for me through every large and small thing in my life. Our two families have lived through many good times together."

Scarpdale nodded in agreement.

"Yes, of course. But you obviously want to say something more - go on man!"

Weatherly lifted his champagne glass, eyed it for a moment, then raised it and met Scarpdale's eyes.

"With the birth of your beautiful child, and as our families are so closely joined, I believe that the next logical step, in order to secure the future of both estates, would be that my son and your daughter become betrothed to one another."

Marcus frowned at his father's words – what did that mean?

For a long minute, there was silence. Then a hoot from Scarpdale as he lifted his own glass.

"What a magnificent idea Weatherly!"

Weatherly grinned widely, set Marcus gently down on the floor, and went to clink his glass with Scarpdale's.

"To the joining of our two families. And may our legacy together prevail!"

Sipping from the champagne, the two friends embraced one another and laughed in triumph, then the Duke of Scarpdale turned to where Marcus stood, and knelt down to ruffle his hair.

"Do you hear that old boy? When you're big enough, you're going to marry my daughter!"

Marcus frowned and looked up at his father, confused.

"What daughter?"

Weatherly smiled down at his son.

"The baby upstairs."

Marcus' eyes widened in shock.

"But it's a girl!"

His protest was met with delight by both Scarpdale and Weatherly, who threw back their heads and laughed.

Marcus didn't think it was funny.

He was supposed to marry a baby? A girl?

And what did it mean to marry anyway?

He huffed and crossed his arms, looking from his father to his father's oldest friend.

Then he looked at Henry and Hawthorne. They didn't seem best pleased either – in fact the Marquess was scowling at the Duke of Scarpdale in a very fierce manner.

Hmm, Marcus thought. He would have to find out what all of this meant. Marry. A girl? A baby? Whatever next?

Adults were strange, sometimes, at least in his opinion.

***

1808

The small girl with the tangle of dark curls toddled across the floor of the parlour towards her father. He watched her approach, his heart aching. It was already clear that, when she grew up, she would be as beautiful as her mother. Sorrow tore through his heart – for her mother would never see her grow.

Just that day, his beloved Charlotte had been laid to rest in the family crypt, stolen from him far too soon by the ravages of unexpected disease.

He gathered the child into his lap, and she looked up at him, a tiny frown creasing her brow.

"Mama...?"

Tears filled his eyes.

He kissed her gently on her furrowed brow.

"Mama has gone to live with God, my Kate, and we will have to make do without her now. But Bessie will help, and I will care for you. I will make sure that you have every chance to be happy, I promise you."

Continued....

I hope that you enjoyed this preview – read the rest at:

https://ariettarichmond.com/go/her-absent-duke

Other Books from Arietta

Books in the
His Majesty's Hounds Series

Books in The Derbyshire Set

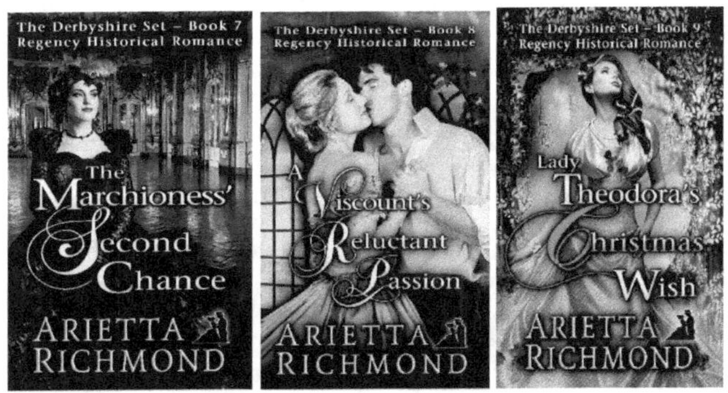

The Marchioness' Second Chance

A Viscount's Reluctant Passion

Lady Theodora's Christmas Wish

The Derbyshire Set Omnibus Edition Vol. 1 (the first three books all in one)

The Derbyshire Set Omnibus Edition Vol. 2 (the second three books all in one)

Regency Collections with Other Authors

Books in the A Duke's Daughters – the Elbury Bouquet Series

A Maiden for a Marquess (Iris) (coming soon)
A Heart for an Heir (Thorne) (coming soon)

Books in the Regency Scandals Series

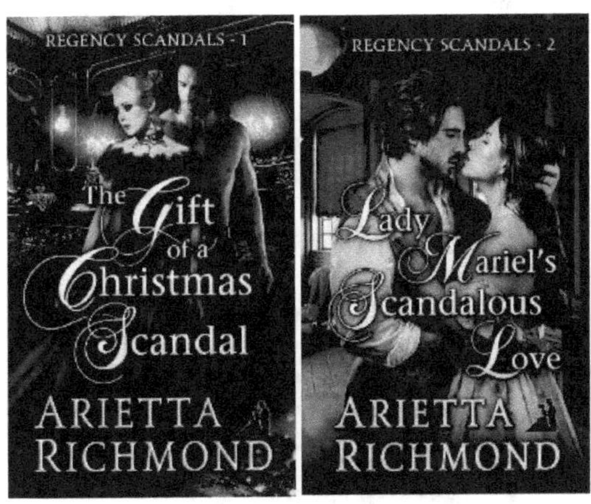

Books in the Nettlefold Chronicles

Books in the Regency Gothic Series

Themed Regency Collections

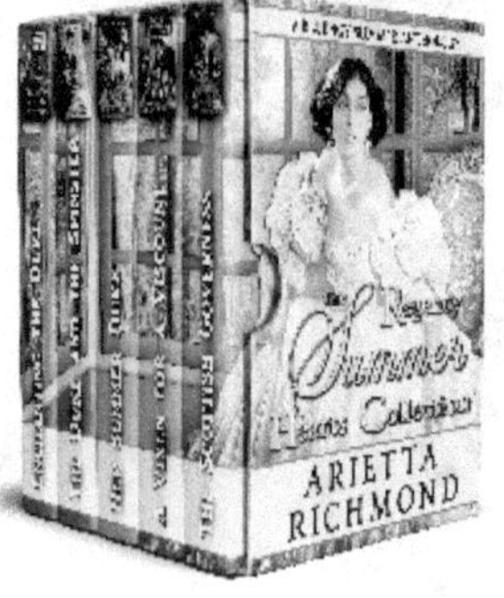

Other Books from Dreamstone Publishing

Dreamstone publishes books in a wide variety of categories ranging from Clean Romance to Erotica, to Kids Books, Books on Writing, Business Books, Photography, Cook Books, Diaries, Coloring books and much more. New books are released each month.

Be the first to know when our next books are coming out

Be first to get all the news – sign up for our newsletter at

https://www.dreamstonepublishing.com